FIC   38749006274266C
PRU   Pruitt, Bernadette.
         True blue

9/08

R.T. JONES MEMORIAL LIBRARY
116 BROWN INDUSTRIAL PKWY
CANTON, GA 30114

D1472616

DISCARD

SEQUOYAH REGIONAL LIBRARY

3 8749 0062 7426 6

TRUE BLUE

TRUE BLUE

BERNADETTE PRUITT

FIVE STAR
A part of Gale, Cengage Learning

GALE
CENGAGE Learning™

Detroit • New York • San Francisco • New Haven, Conn • Waterville, Maine • London

PROPERTY OF
SEQUOYAH REGIONAL
LIBRARY SYSTEM

GALE
CENGAGE Learning

Copyright © 2008 by Bernadette Pruitt.
Five Star Publishing, a part of Gale, Cengage Learning.

ALL RIGHTS RESERVED
This novel is a work of fiction. Names, characters, places and incidents are either the product of the author's imagination, or, if real, used fictitiously.

No part of this work covered by the copyright herein may be reproduced, transmitted, stored, or used in any form or by any means graphic, electronic, or mechanical, including but not limited to photocopying, recording, scanning, digitizing, taping, Web distribution, information networks, or information storage and retrieval systems, except as permitted under Section 107 or 108 of the 1976 United States Copyright Act, without the prior written permission of the publisher.

The publisher bears no responsibility for the quality of information provided through author or third-party Web sites and does not have any control over, nor assume any responsibility for, information contained in these sites. Providing these sites should not be construed as an endorsement or approval by the publisher of these organizations or of the positions they may take on various issues.

Set in 11 pt. Plantin.
Printed on permanent paper.

LIBRARY OF CONGRESS CATALOGING-IN-PUBLICATION DATA

Pruitt, Bernadette.
  True blue / Bernadette Pruitt. — 1st ed.
    p. cm.
  ISBN-13: 978-1-59414-701-2 (hardcover : alk. paper)
  ISBN-10: 1-59414-701-9 (hardcover : alk. paper)
  I. Title.
PS3566.R823T78 2008
813'.54—dc22
                                        2008016369

First Edition. First Printing: August 2008.
Published in 2008 in conjunction with Tekno Books.

Printed in the United States of America
1 2 3 4 5 6 7 12 11 10 09 08

TRUE BLUE

CHAPTER ONE

Drake Matthieson had three goals in life: to be a good cop, to land a record-breaking trout, and to avoid marriage.

For thirty-six years, he had successfully dodged the latter. If commendations counted for anything, he was among the best of Denver's finest. Now, on the eve of his first vacation in years, he was going after that trout. He ran a towel over a thick crop of dark, wet hair, pulled on a navy blue police t-shirt and tucked it into a pair of faded jeans. Then he stepped up to the police locker room's steamy mirror and gave himself a critical inspection. His eyes were underscored with fatigue. There was a raw scrape on one cheek. His face was wreathed with a day's growth of dark stubble. It was the face of a man who deserved a rest.

Shortly before three that morning, he and four other members of the SWAT team had ramrodded their way into a house, surprising an escaped convict and the woman who was harboring him. After toting them off to jail, he'd put in four hours of overtime, followed by two miles of jogging around the department's fitness track.

Not that he was complaining. He loved the adrenalin-spiked life he led. Doing something different every day. Helping to bring about justice. But in a line of work that demanded razor-sharp senses, a man couldn't afford to lose his edge. He turned a cheek to the mirror and ran his fingers over the angular outline of his jaw. Alone on the Killarney River, he could forget about shaving for a week. Maybe he could forget some other things, too.

With the renewed energy of a man eagerly anticipating a week that would be completely his own, to do whatever he pleased, he tossed his duffel bag over his shoulder and strode out the door.

Hadley Spencer looked both ways, although the light was clearly green, before proceeding through Mountain Spring, Colorado's last major intersection. In the back seat was her two-year-old son, Nicky, strapped into the sturdiest child seat available. In the front seat was a portfolio case containing work for several of her graphic design clients. For one client, there was a draft of a restaurant advertisement, for another were several proposals for a corporate logo.

She'd come to the outlying Denver suburb a year ago to be near one of her few relatives, Aunt Margaret, who was seventy going on seventeen. Hadley's intentions were to look after her while starting a new life of her own. But, as it turned out, Aunt Margaret looked out for herself quite nicely, flitting from one cruise or bus tour to the next, and meeting some nice old gentlemen along the way. Just yesterday, she'd sent Hadley a postcard from Phoenix where a retired vacuum cleaner executive had treated her to a Margarita.

All things considered, she'd settled well into the small mountain town. It was near enough to Denver to establish a modest client base and far enough away to provide relative safety and calm. Mountain Spring was an old-fashioned town of picket fences and rose trellises. Houses with porch swings and screen doors that caught cool, summer breezes. It was a monument to simpler times, simplicity being what Hadley needed most in her life.

She followed the winding ribbon of highway leading into the

outer rim of Denver's mile-high sprawl. The mountains undulated against a clear spring sky, their purple-shadowed beauty placing her under a spell. It was at the police division headquarters just inside the Denver city limits where the spell always broke. The gray stucco building, with its flags snapping in the wind and parking lot full of cruisers reminded her of the husband she'd lost.

She increased her speed, quickly reducing the building to a small image in her rearview mirror. She had two clients waiting for her. And she had an odd twinge in her right side.

She ignored it at first. Hoisting a growing toddler about was bound to create strains and sprains. But now, it was getting harder to ignore, like a clock ticking slowly in her abdomen.

Hadley shut it out during the next few hours as she got approval of the restaurant ad, and delivered several drafts of a logo to an advertising agency. But on the way home, the twinge in her side escalated into one relentless stabbing pain. In the rearview mirror, she saw her blond bangs had dampened and now stuck to her forehead. Her eyes were dull with pain.

Her body bore the added burden of fear. She glanced to the back seat where Nicky was engrossed in the pursuit of untying one of his sneakers. She had to get home. Just ten more miles.

She found it increasingly difficult to focus on driving as the pain tightened its grip on her. The steering wheel slickened beneath her palms. She rolled down the window slightly and took in gulps of cool, fresh air.

It was the last jolt of pain that almost sent her over the edge. Struggling to swallow the moans rising in her throat, she doubled over, striking her chin hard against the steering wheel. There was no getting around it: she wasn't going to make it home. She needed help. Now!

Suddenly, she was desperate for the sprawling, gray building with all the police cars to appear over the horizon. She was almost there, praying she could hold on just another mile or so. When it finally came into view, she turned into the parking lot so abruptly that the minivan's tires squealed. An officer emerging from the building with a duffel bag slung over his shoulder looked up. As she drove toward him, another bolt of pain pierced her side, causing her to cry out. The car weaved. The last thing she remembered was groping for the brake.

Drake watched a dark green minivan creep unsteadily into the lot, then come to a clumsy stop, a front wheel jumping the curb. The car was angled so awkwardly that it took up two parking spaces and part of the sidewalk.

It wasn't often that a drunk drove up to the station to turn himself in, but such things had been known to happen. But on second glance, it was clear that there was more to this case than one too many for the road.

As he approached the car, the door opened and a blonde, clutching her midsection, stumbled out. Drake rushed up and caught her under the arms just as her knees started to buckle.

"Pain," she groaned. "I need medical help. Please hurry."

The only color in her face came from thickly lashed eyes the color of a summer sky. They were clouded with fear.

"Get back in the car and lie down," he said, gently easing her back into the car. "I'll call for an ambulance. Take some deep breaths and try to keep still."

He sprinted back into the station, yelling out a medical emergency code number, and then ran back to her. Despite his orders to the contrary, she was sitting up again, rocking back and forth, her arms cradling her midsection.

"Help's on the way," he said. "Hang in there. You're going to be OK" He adjusted the seat into a reclining position and gently nudged her against it. He felt her resistance in his fingertips.

"The baby," she said breathlessly. "Please take care of Nicky."

Drake glanced into the back seat to find a sturdy blond boy with eyes even bluer than his mother's. He looked at Drake with interest, babbled something unintelligible and proudly held out a soggy shoelace.

"Don't worry about him. He'll be fine." His own voice fell back on his ears as dispassionate, almost cold, compared to the underlying desperation in hers. Strong emotion was a luxury he didn't allow himself.

"Where does it hurt exactly?"

She pointed to her right side.

He touched a hand to her forehead, its heat telegraphing instantly to his fingertips. He'd had enough first-aid training to know that she could be in serious trouble. All signs pointed to an appendix that could blow at any time. Where in blazes were the paramedics?

Two more cops appeared, one with bottled water, and another with a pillow. A young corporal got in on the passenger side and slid the pillow under her head.

"You're in good hands," he reassured her. "They don't come any better than Matthieson here."

The other officer, a kid fresh out of the academy, uncapped the bottle and handed it to Drake.

"Thanks, guys," he said. "I know we're shorthanded today, so if you need to get back to work, I can handle it from here."

They disappeared, one of them pausing first to pat the kid on the knee.

Drake stood close by as the mother sipped weakly from the bottle. With a whispered "thank you," she handed it back to him, and collapsed against the seat.

"Hold on," he said. "It won't be long."

Her eyes were murky. They were beautiful eyes, nonetheless, wide and round. Her hair was short and tousled, her face heart-

11

shaped. A pointed chin gave her a slightly elfin appearance. Then he noticed what looked like the start of a nasty bruise on it. She wasn't a beauty in the classical sense. But she was strikingly appealing in a fresh, girl-next-door sort of way. Alarmed by his sudden impulse to brush her bangs away from her forehead, he stepped back slightly.

Drake glanced nervously into the back seat. He didn't know anything about babies except that they wreaked a lot of havoc, so he wasn't in a position to judge this one's age. All he could surmise was that he was big enough to walk, and therefore demolish anything that got in his way.

"Can you give me a phone number for your husband or someone we can contact?" he asked.

Her eyes darkened. "No husband—widow."

Drake inwardly flinched. In the distance, a siren began to wail.

"Other family?"

"Aunt Margaret. On bus tour."

The siren, warbling and shrill, was now upon them. The ambulance pulled into the lot in a spin of flashing lights, its siren growling to a stop. Doors flew open and paramedics appeared, snapping a gurney into position and rushing it toward them.

Drake squeezed in another question: "A baby-sitter?"

"Not home."

A knot of frustration formed in his chest. "It's all right. We'll find someone to take care of the boy," he assured her.

"You . . ." she said.

His gut reacted with a hard twist. She crumpled over in pain. He couldn't tell her that he wasn't in any position to baby-sit. And she was in no position to be questioned any further.

They gently lifted her onto the gurney and whisked her away. The next thing he knew, he was looking at a fading set of ambulance taillights and a kid who was suddenly bawling his lungs out. Panic wasn't an emotion he indulged in, but there it was, chewing at the pit of his stomach.

She couldn't have meant that she wanted him personally to take care of the kid, he told himself. She was delirious. He was married to his work, all right, but his job description didn't include being an off-duty nanny. He thought of the clock ticking away on his vacation—the solitude of the forest, the soothing sounds of the river. He had to get this situation under control—fast.

"Calm down, little guy," he said to the toddler as he got into the car. The order was ignored.

Hurriedly and with skill, Drake backed the vehicle off the sidewalk, parked it neatly in a single space and yanked the keys out of the ignition. He slid open the side door and extracted the baby from his seat, handling him like an egg with a particularly thin shell. He grabbed a briefcase and a bag imprinted with teddy bears, and went inside the station.

Sgt. Jake Brockman looked up from his desk, cocking an eyebrow in surprise. "You're supposed to be on vacation, pal."

"I've got a little problem here. The mother was the medical emergency I just reported and there doesn't seem to be any nearby relatives available to take the baby."

The older man stroked a jaw. "None?"

"None that I can determine at this point. She said something about me taking the kid, so she must have been pretty desperate. If you wouldn't mind watching him for a moment, I'll see if I can get any more information from her personal things."

"Sure, Lieutenant."

Drake quickly and eagerly handed the boy over to the sergeant. "I owe you."

While the sergeant, a grandfather several times over, tried to soothe him by bouncing him on his knee, Drake unzipped the

13

brown leather briefcase. He pulled out a hard folder and yanked off the string that bound it. A quick look revealed what appeared to be some sort of advertising material. He put it back, then checked an inside pocket. There, he found what he was looking for: a wallet.

He flipped it open. Clearly displayed was a Colorado driver's license identifying her as Hadley Spencer. A quick mental calculation showed her to be twenty-seven. She lived in one of the Mountain Spring neighborhoods he'd patrolled as a rookie, one that he remembered as having homes that were old and modest, yet rich in character. And although driver's license photos were notoriously unflattering, the bad angle, cheap lens, and poor lighting had failed to dim her bright and wholesome good looks. Drake studied the photo for a moment with considerable appreciation before continuing his search for next-of-kin.

He fanned through the photo section of the wallet, working through baby pictures from the bottom up. When he reached the second picture from the top, his hand froze. The man in the photo was about thirty, strong-jawed and with closely cropped light brown hair. He was dressed in a police uniform. On his sleeve was the patch of the Dallas Police Department. Drake could tell from the square set of his shoulders that he wore it proudly. He slipped the photo out of its sleeve and turned it over. On the back was scrawled: "To Hadley with all my love, Quint." He felt a twist in his gut. Was this man the baby's father? Had he heard her right? Widow?

Drake fumbled through the rest of the wallet, but came up with nothing but a dry-cleaning ticket, nine dollars and some odd change.

His search through the woman's personal effects had been so intense that it was only now that he noticed that the baby had quit crying. He looked up and saw that the sergeant had the kid sitting on the floor and drinking happily from a spouted cup that he must have extracted from the baby bag.

"Any luck?" he asked.

"Not really," Drake answered dispiritedly. He handed him her driver's license. "Run this through and see what you can come up with."

The sergeant tapped in the license number. Drake watched over his shoulder as the information slowly materialized on the computer screen. Next of kin: Margaret Barrymore, Mountain Spring.

Drake grabbed the phone and punched in her number. After the tenth ring, there was still no answer.

"That's what I was afraid of," he said, hanging up. "This must be the aunt who's on a bus tour."

Drake pulled the picture of the officer out of her wallet. "Looks like this might have been her husband. Check him out with Dallas PD. See about any other relatives."

Sgt. Brockman punched a few more computer keys, then picked up the phone. Drake could tell by the sound of the conversation that things weren't going well.

"What did you find out?" he asked nervously as Brockman hung up.

"He was her husband all right," he said darkly. "Killed in the line of duty."

Drake winced.

"The only other next of kin listed was his father, who's stationed overseas in the military."

Drake took a moment to pull his wits together.

"You don't suppose your wife would mind a little baby-sitting tonight, do you?"

"Not if she was at home. She's in South Dakota visiting her sister," he said, jumping up to answer the telephone. "Looks like we might have to contact the authorities."

15

"We *are* the authorities, Sarge."

The sergeant was interrupted by the phone again at which point the baby dropped his cup and toddled toward a rubber plant. Drake grabbed him just as he was about to topple it. He set the boy back on the floor, put the cup back in his hand, and stuck the plant up on the sergeant's desk.

The sergeant hung up again. "I meant the child welfare authorities," he said. "They should be able to get somebody lined up by morning."

Drake's breath stalled. "Morning?"

Brockman nodded slowly. "There's a shortage of licensed foster parents."

The baby dropped his cup again and began to fuss.

"I'll take him over to the hospital," Drake said finally. "Surely there's a sitter or some kind of provisions."

"Good idea," he said, reaching for the phone again. "I'd watch him myself, but things are too hectic here. Besides, didn't she intimate she wanted *you* to take care of him?" There was a mischievous twinkle in his eye. Drake's earlier reputation as a ladies' man had been slow to die.

Drake cast him a chiding look. "Now that I think of it, she probably meant 'you' in the collective sense, as in police."

"Um hmmm," he said, cradling the receiver on his shoulder.

Drake sucked in a deep breath. Whatever she meant, the woman had no easily discernible next of kin. There she was, probably under the knife at this moment. And here he was under the gun—figuratively, at least.

He looked at the boy and the boy looked back at him as if they were from different planets. The baby's lower lip had an ominous set to it as if he were going to crumple into tears at any moment. He suddenly looked very small, even in Brockman's cracker box of an office. The kid was frightened, bewildered, and Drake realized with a twinge, absolutely helpless. On top of all that, he was the child of one of their own—a police officer.

His mother was going to be waking up in a hospital bed worrying about him. The way things looked, she was going to be waking up alone. He looked at his watch and heaved a sigh. It was almost seven o'clock. He thought of the Killarney River and the silver flash of trout. But it was duty, not the fish that called. The Killarney was going to have to wait because it looked like he was the only one there for Hadley Spencer.

Hadley awoke around midnight in a white haze of confusion. Then, piece by piece, a picture formed: hospital, lights, siren. Her desperate attempt to make it to the police station. Nicky.

Her heart leaped. She mouthed her child's name. She tried to reach out for him but her arm wouldn't move.

"He's fine. Don't worry." The voice coming from the side of her bed was rich, resonant and very male. "Aren't you going to ask about yourself?"

She turned her head to see a sharpening image of the officer from the police station. He placed a hand on her arm. Although his touch was gentle, there was an underlying strength to it.

He was tall and fit, an inch or two over six feet with neatly squared and powerful shoulders. His hair, as black and glossy as onyx, was closely cropped at the sides, leaving glints of silver exposed at his temples. The top, not much longer, was in slight disarray. He had a straight nose and a strong chin marked by a small, but prominent scar just under the curve of his bottom lip. His face was a mask of objectivity and composure, but his impassive expression failed to distract from his striking good looks.

His eyes, a piercing gray, offered little insight into the man within. Hadley understood how dealing with humanity at its worst could take the sparkle out of a man's eyes. She knew something about the dark side of life herself.

Suddenly, she became aware of a dull, pulling sensation and reached for her side.

"They took your appendix out," he explained. "Just in time, I might add. You're going to be fine."

Hadley's sigh of relief was followed by a jolt. "Where's Nicky?"

"Asleep in the hospital's day care center. I asked them to bring him to you when he wakes up."

"Thank you so much." Her voice was wobbly with relief. "I'm so glad he's in good hands."

Drake swallowed hard. "I'm afraid they were only able to take him on an emergency basis. We need to find someone else to care for him as soon as possible. Do you have anyone we can contact?"

Hadley felt a hollow sensation in her chest. Unable to take care of her own child, she was brought face to face with a raw vulnerability almost as frightening as what she had experienced three years ago.

She took a deep breath to clear her mind. "My Aunt Margaret is on a bus tour in Arizona."

Drake's mouth, still framed by the stubble he hadn't had time to shave off, tightened into a firm line.

"What about friends?"

"We're fairly new here."

"Any other baby-sitters?"

"Just Kelly from across the street. She's out of town, too. I'm not sure when she's supposed to be back."

His chest, deep and muscular, rose and fell under his faded denim shirt, but the cool objectivity in his eyes remained unchanged. "I'll check on her."

Hadley nodded, but with effort. Kelly, who lived with her parents and was a freshman at the local junior college, was very capable and Nicky liked her. The problem was that it was spring break.

"By the way, I'm Lieutenant Matthieson. Just call me Drake," he said crisply.

"I'm Hadley—Hadley Spencer."

"I know—from your personal effects."

She nodded. Of course. That's how they did things.

"Don't worry about your belongings. They're secure," he said. "And, if you need me, the people at the nurse's station have my number." Without another word, he turned toward the door.

"Wait . . . please," she said, struggling to get up. She tried to ignore the sharp pull in her abdomen.

With a couple of long, quick steps, he was back at her bedside. "Hey, take it easy," he said, nudging her gently back on the pillow.

"I just wanted to thank you again," she said.

He responded with a fleeting, almost awkward touch of her arm, and then left the room.

Hadley listened as the sound of his steps faded into the din and distance of the hospital corridor. She placed her fingers over the spot where his fingers had been and, with alarm, felt her pulse quicken. It was too bad this guardian angel wore a badge.

It was barely seven in the morning and Drake was already on his way to Kelly's house. Should he be graced by a miracle, little Nicky would be in his sitter's arms and he'd be on his way to the Killarney by noon. He came to an abrupt stop in front of a small but solid-looking English-style cottage with an arched doorway. Ivy climbed up the brick façade. He gave the door a couple of urgent raps with a tarnished brass knocker. A door opened, but it was the door of the next house. A wisp of an old lady, eighty if a minute, came out on the porch and studied him suspiciously. As he approached her, he pulled out his police identification card. "I'm looking for Kelly or her family," he said.

"She hasn't gotten herself in trouble, has she? That younger generation is just asking for it."

"No, ma'am. I wanted to see her about baby-sitting."

"They'll be back at the end of the week," she said. "They went to the slopes—the whole family."

Thanking her, Drake jumped back in his Jeep. So much for miracles, he murmured disheartedly. Pulling his cell phone off his belt, he punched in the number of Grace Montgomery, retired policewoman. Despite her hard-boiled exterior, she was a sucker for kids. She'd baby-sit for a day or so.

He got her on the first ring. As luck would have it, she was just on her way out the door to catch a flight to Acapulco. Adios. His heart sank like a rock. Why couldn't Hadley Spencer have relatives like everybody else? Then it struck him with painful recall: he didn't have much of a family either, and what was left of it wouldn't have inspired a Norman Rockwell painting. An invisible cinch tightened around his chest. He had to act fast or the reservation on his cabin would be canceled. He called the station again. Child Welfare *might* have someone available by tomorrow morning.

He got back in the car and dropped his head against the headrest. Maybe he could talk the hospital into keeping Nicky until then. What a pathetic optimist he was.

He thought of the swirling crystal waters of the Killarney, but the image was quickly replaced by Hadley Spencer's golden hair in disarray against her pillow. He imagined the feel of it, soft as a spring rain, against his fingers.

He sat up suddenly, frightened by the way she churned up his emotions, emotions he'd long kept in check. It was caused by the precious few hours of sleep he'd gotten. Had to be.

Throughout her ordeal, he'd observed, she'd been fiercely maternal. She would have somehow gotten out of bed, stitches popping and IV dragging, to protect her child if she'd had to. But in the meantime, she had put her trust in a group of blue-uniformed men, who, truth be known, could pin an armed robber to the ground easier than they could pin a diaper on a baby.

But that's what she wanted. She didn't want her child turned over to just anyone and just anyone was what you might get when you turned a kid over to Child Welfare. Not that there weren't good foster parents, but despite the best intentions of the state, a few were just in it for the money, what little of it there was. He knew about that from personal experience.

His thoughts went back to his own childhood and of being passed, unwanted, from one relative to another after his parents died. He'd felt so alone, much like Hadley Spencer must be feeling right now. He shifted uncomfortably behind the steering wheel, not liking where this train of thought was taking him.

Being a cop was part of a brotherhood, an extended family that literally depended on each other for survival. That seemed to be the way Hadley Spencer looked at it, too. Given that, what kind of officer would he be to let her down?

Well, drat, he'd take the kid for a day or so, heaven help the hapless babe.

CHAPTER TWO

Accepting help wasn't easy for Hadley. She had learned fast that a partner in life, someone to fall back on, is anything but guaranteed. She'd learned to rely on her inner resources, to do for herself.

The emergency surgery had shaken her, making it clear that she wasn't the 'iron lady' after all. Just give her a day, a few quarts of the broth and juice that they doled out on the hour, and she'd be back on her feet. She didn't like needing people. She didn't like needing Drake Matthieson, in particular.

She finished the rest of her broth, a concoction that tasted slightly of the can from which it probably came, and she willed herself to be well. She had a police officer to dispatch back to his division and a toddler to take care of.

There was a soft tap on the door.

"Lieutenant Matthieson here." His tone was crisp and official.

She quickly pulled up the sheet and tucked it around her. "Come in."

The door swung open and Drake appeared in full uniform. Nicky was sitting in the crook of his arm. Hadley's heart leapt at the sight of the boy. Instantly forgetting her worries, she held out her arms. Almost before Drake could set him down on the bed, she enfolded him into an embrace. "How's the world's best boy?" she asked, nuzzling her cheek against his head.

He gave her a toothy grin. Other than the fact he was wearing the same overalls and long-sleeved t-shirt as the day before, he appeared none the worse for the experience. His dark blue eyes sparkled, even.

"You've got a sitter, now," Drake said.

Hadley's spirits lifted. "Kelly's back?"

"No."

Perplexed, she studied his face. He was cleanly shaven now, the small, white scar clearly exposed on his chin. Despite the stark, knife-edged crispness of his uniform and a bearing of understated authority, this was not a man who sat behind a desk. Drake Matthieson was a hands-on, in-the-trenches cop. She'd developed a feel for such things.

"Who is it, then?"

"Me."

Her lips parted in surprise. "But I can't ask you to do that."

"You already did."

Her mind spun. "I didn't really mean you personally. I meant . . ." She sighed deeply. "I don't know what I meant."

He ran a hand through his hair. "Look, I've gone through the roster—a retired policewoman, a cop's wife, Kelly. Even Child Welfare can't take him right away, especially since he hardly fits into the category of being abused or neglected. On short notice, I'm pretty much all that's left."

"Do you have children?"

He shook his head. "Nope. That usually takes a wife, which I haven't got."

Hadley pulled Nicky closer to her.

"Look, I know I'm no Mary Poppins, but I've had some experience at this."

"Have you?" The trepidation in her voice was all too thinly disguised.

"I was a baby once myself."

Hadley looked at him with incredulity, and then laughed.

Her stitches pulled hard enough to make her wince. This was insane, but she was hardly in a position to refuse. How could she?

"You checked again with the hospital day care?"

"I did," he said quickly. "That's why you see me in uniform. It usually gets me what I want. Only, this time it didn't. State regulations, they said. Only so many kids per childcare worker are allowed. Nicky's been evicted."

Hadley took a deep breath and let it out slowly. "Lieutenant, I don't want you to think I'm not grateful. I really am."

"You're just nervous, right? Well, don't worry about a thing. Nick and I will watch a little baseball, catch up on our reading, and do the things that guys do."

Hadley looked at him warily. "Don't forget that he's only two years old. You can't exactly turn on the sports channel and toss him a can of beer."

"A carton of milk, then. I'll read him stories."

"That sounds nice," she conceded.

"Got any other advice?"

"He eats junior foods."

"What are those?"

"They're for older babies who can chew. There's plenty in the pantry. He'll eat everything but the carrots. And another thing: He grabs hold of everything in sight. Try to keep things out of his reach."

"I can handle that."

Hadley felt a stab of guilt. He really had no idea.

"Another thing: He's an early bird. He's up by six—five-thirty sometimes."

"No problem," he said, sounding like a man very much in charge. Yet she couldn't help but notice that the circles under his eyes seemed to be darkening by the minute.

"And you might have to go to the grocery store to pick up a

few items," she said, casting him an apologetic look. "It seems I was getting low on milk. Nicky also likes bananas. And . . ." She hated to keep adding *and*'s. She was already imposing more than he knew. "He's in potty training, but you don't need to worry about that. Just keep him in diapers."

She thought she saw his tawny skin go pale. "And, if any of my clients call, please tell them what happened and that I'll get back with them as soon as I can. The hospital is releasing me tomorrow."

"What sort of clients?" he asked.

A policeman's suspicion never took a rest, it seemed. "I'm a graphic artist. I work at home. That way I can care for Nicky myself."

"I'll be spending the night in your house, right?"

She thought of the glowing review the young officer at the station had given Drake. After all, he was a cop, and he'd be there for just one night.

"It would be best, if you wouldn't mind. His crib and all of his things are there. He'll settle right in. He's really a good boy. Honest."

Nicky tossed the buzzer off her bed. It hit the bedside table, knocking off a box of tissues. Drake put it back and handed Hadley the buzzer.

"I can't tell you how much I appreciate this," she repeated. "I'm so sorry to have to inconvenience you."

"There's nothing to be sorry about. I just happen to be on vacation this week anyway."

Hadley bit her bottom lip. He must have had other plans, but she wasn't sure if she wanted to hear about them. She already felt guilty enough. "The key to the house is on the same ring as the car keys. It's the brass one."

Drake took the keys from his pocket and tossed them into the air with confidence. "We're on our way."

She kissed the top of the baby's head and gave him a lingering hug before Drake lifted him off the bed. By all indications there was nothing to worry about. Someone who would give up part of his vacation to help a person in need had to have his heart in the right place. But she worried anyway. When it came to Nicky, she'd always worry.

He carried him out the door as effortlessly as if he were a doll, leaving her with an empty space in her heart the size of Texas.

With the radio tuned to the fishing report, Drake set off for Hadley's house on Aspen Street. As luck would have it, the trout were practically spilling over the banks. In the back seat, Nicky howled. Drake glanced into the rearview mirror. The kid's face was as red as the proverbial beet.

He remembered once, on an all-night stakeout, he had to sit in a sweltering van, made even hotter by the fact that he was wearing a bulletproof vest and headgear. There were four of them crammed inside. They'd forgotten to bring water and one guy had neglected to put on deodorant. But in that strange way that only cops would understand, they were having fun. How he longed to be on a stakeout like that right now.

"Hey, little pal," he said, glancing into the rearview mirror. "We're almost there."

The baby switched over to a hiccuping wail that made it sound as if he were in imminent danger of drowning in his own tears.

There had to be a little bit of a saint in every mother, Drake figured. Too bad he never really got to know his own. In these last moments, he'd come to appreciate what an awesome responsibility Hadley Spencer had. She was on duty twenty-four hours a day, seven days a week with no backup. On top of that, she symbolized every cop's worst nightmare—the widow left to raise his child alone. Drake had made up his mind long ago that he wasn't going to risk leaving anyone behind. He knew first-hand what that was like.

In desperation, Drake started to sing.

> *Hey, little cowboy*
> *Hang up your hat*
> *Kick off your boots*
> *It's time for a nap . . .*

> *Rest easy little cowboy*
> *Everything will be fine*
> *Ride off in the sunset,*
> *Leave your troubles behind.*

He'd learned the tune from an old girlfriend who had composed the song for her nephew. She was a voice major. Some voice. Some legs. He was a baritone, she'd told him, and he wasn't bad at all. They'd had something special going for a while, but she wanted more than he could give her. Most of them did.

Nicky choked himself into silence and fixed his gaze on the back of Drake's head. Encouraged, Drake kept on singing until he turned onto Aspen Street.

Hadley's house was a small 20s-era gray clapboard bungalow with white trim and a porch that spanned the width of it. The front door was a shiny, dark green and there were lace curtains at the windows. It looked a literal factory of domesticity, the kind of place where a woman made her own piecrusts. Drake brought his Jeep to a halt in the driveway and got the baby out.

"Here we are, bud," he said, carrying him up the steps. "We'll order a pizza, then kick back a bit. What do you say?"

"Mom-my."

"Believe me, I wish she was here, too."

Drake noticed a swing on the front porch, along with clay pots of pansies clustered on each side of the front door. Despite what she'd been through, it was obvious that Hadley still found pleasure in the little things in life, and he couldn't help but be stirred by that.

Suddenly, he was stirred by something else—something warm and wet on the front of his uniform. "Mayday!" he uttered, quickly putting the boy down. He jammed the key in the lock, threw open the deadbolt and tore through the house in search of diapers. He found a box of them next to the crib in the back bedroom.

It occurred to him that in all of his thirty-six years, sixteen of them spent as a police officer, he'd done many things, from hog-tying suspects to rescuing a kitten from a manhole. But he'd never changed a diaper.

He ripped it out of the box, dismayed to see that it was the next to the last one and tossed it on the floor. Then he laid the baby down, fumbling at snaps and buttons until finally giving up and yanking the denim overalls completely off. Apparently thinking it was all a game, Nicky started kicking wildly, catching Drake on the chin with his heel. Surprised, Drake managed to grab his ankles long enough to rip off the sodden diaper. But in the split second it took him to reach for the fresh one, his captive bolted.

"Freeze!" he yelled after the bare bottom disappearing into the hallway. The call went unheeded.

Drake scrambled after him, his foot accidentally squishing into the discarded diaper, and plucked the boy up off the living room floor. Nicky giggled, showing off several sparkling teeth.

"You know, you could get five years for this," Drake said, carrying him back into the bedroom. "It's called resisting arrest. Now, let's get back down to business."

After a couple of attempts, he managed to tape the diaper on.

It was somewhat lopsided, but who was going to know? He tossed the wet overalls in the shower and let water run over them for a few moments. After he managed to get a fresh pair on the kid, Drake was overcome by a wave of raw exhaustion. In the last two days, he'd had hardly any sleep. While he was barely able to stand, the kid was just hitting his stride.

Drake looked at his watch. It was barely four o'clock but it seemed much later. "Where's the telephone?" he asked, not expecting an answer.

Nicky toddled over to a box of toys in the corner and proudly dragged out a yellow plastic phone, the receiver dangling by a string. Drake found himself grinning in spite of himself. "Thanks, but you keep it. That's your private line."

Drake found the real phone in the kitchen and ordered a large pizza with extra pepperoni. In the cabinet, he rummaged for something for Nicky and found a jar of chicken and noodles. He dumped it into a bowl and stuck it in the microwave. He plopped the baby in his high chair and strapped him in.

The boy ate hungrily and without incident except for sticking a hand in the dish and wiping it off on Drake's shirt. It occurred to him at that point that the high chair made a good holding pen so he grabbed an assortment of toys and set them on the tray. While he waited for the pizza, he took a quick stroll through the house.

The living room had a nice, plump sofa with a rumpled gray slipcover and needlework pillows. There was an old, oak rocking chair with a frayed blue baby blanket tossed over the back and a floral-print rug that left the borders of the shiny oak floor exposed. The fireplace was filled with candles and above the mantel were four watercolors in gilded frames. He paused to study them. Depicted in a lively, blurred style was the same mountain scene captured in each of the four seasons. In the corner of each, in neat letters, was Hadley's signature. Drake usually paid little attention to such things, but this room had an effect on him. It was feminine, restful and soothing on the nerves. And it smelled nice, like a freshly cut orange.

He'd barely stepped into the doorway of Hadley Spencer's bedroom when the baby started to cry and the doorbell rang. The baby was crying because he'd thrown all his toys overboard. The doorbell was ringing because the pizza had arrived. Drake hastily took care of both.

He switched on the television set, deposited the baby and the toys on the floor and sank wearily into the sofa with the pizza carton on his lap. No cable, it seemed. No sports channel. He settled for a special on manatees. When Nicky got restless, he quieted him with bits of pizza.

He wasn't sure how it happened, but after he'd polished off the pizza and a soft drink, he fell asleep. He didn't even realize it until he awoke with a start to find Nicky snoozing on the rug. A cold sweat broke out over him and his heart started to pound when he thought of how the kid could have drowned in the toilet or crawled in the oven. After all, he was supposed to be there to serve and protect.

His knees wobbling as if he'd just dodged a bullet, he took advantage of the baby's semi-comatose state to put a fresh diaper on him and put him in his crib. Too tired to even take a shower, he plodded down the hallway to Hadley's bedroom, stripped down to his boxers and collapsed onto her bed. It smelled faintly of spring flowers and melting snow. It smelled like her.

Hadley Spencer was softness and strength, a rose and a rock. She was a survivor. There was evidence of that in every room in the house, from the healthy, slumbering baby to the original artwork on the wall. That she could turn the chaos and sadness of life into such beauty and order struck him as nothing short of amazing.

He'd hate to leave a woman like Hadley behind, even if she could lift the earth on her shoulder like a female Atlas. And as he lay in her bed, he reaffirmed the promise he made to himself long ago—to steer clear of strong emotional attachments. But he couldn't help thinking of the gentle curve of her cheek and eyes as blue as a morning glory.

He sat up. Nope, he couldn't sleep here. It stirred up his imagination too much. Dragging off the extra quilt draped over the foot of the four-poster bed, he strode into the living room. He gathered up a couple of needlepoint cushions for his head and flopped down on the sofa.

He closed his eyes. Now he was too wired to sleep. He pressed the illumination button on the watch he'd forgotten to take off. It was 11:16. Light from a street lamp flickered over a wall. The refrigerator hummed. But the real distraction was his own heart, strumming like an idling motor. Mountain Spring, where he had spent his early years as a cop, was a cache of memories. Now, in the still of night, they were rushing at him all at once.

On this very street, he'd investigated the disappearance of an entire flowerbed, picked clean of prize-winning irises. It turned out to be the work of a jealous garden-club rival. He'd helped firemen fish a four-year-old out of a manhole, and caught three kids who had been shooting out streetlights all over town with their B-B guns. He'd rounded up two old men who had slipped out of a nursing home to go on one last fling. It was a smaller, quieter town then, innocent almost. The disappearance of Callie Murphy had changed that.

Callie Murphy was a 16-year-old misfit who seemingly vanished in broad daylight. It would soon be five years since she was reported missing. There was still no sign of her. He knew because he'd kept up with the case. He had a soft spot for confused and troubled kids.

A rebellious girl with a head of wild strawberry blond curls, she wore her non-conformity like a badge. There were two things that set her apart from her classmates: an artistic talent which exceeded anything her teacher had ever seen on a high school level and her strange clothing.

Forays to vintage clothing shops and the Salvation Army had yielded an extensive retro wardrobe. One day she might be wearing a jacket from an Army dress uniform over jeans, the next a Sixties mini-skirt with knee-high boots. Whatever she wore was usually topped off with black lipstick and nail polish. That she would mar an attractive face in such a way made no sense to Drake. It was the Army coat, complete with military patches, that she had been wearing on the day he had picked her up for driving ten miles an hour over the speed limit. She'd let him know in no uncertain terms what she thought of it. She ripped the ticket in two right in front of his eyes.

One day, a Denver TV station had come to town to cover a murder case that had ended up in Mountain Spring because of a change of venue. When the regular courtroom artist became ill, Drake had suggested that the station approach Callie. She performed with her usual artistic excellence and later even thanked him. A few weeks after that, she disappeared.

Callie was the kind of girl who could well have gone stomping off somewhere just to make a statement. On the other hand, her disappearance never made sense. First of all, she'd left behind her car, a bright yellow Volkswagen Beetle. She'd also left unfinished a variety of projects that she was doing for a regional high school art show. Other than her parents, no one was more shocked than her art teacher.

Callie had come from what appeared to be a stable middle-class family. Her stepfather ran a car dealership that his family owned and he served on the board of the Chamber of Commerce. Mr. Clean it seemed. But as an only child, Callie had been close to her natural father, who had died just months before her mother married Stuart Wycliff. Put that on top of an artistic temperament and Drake could see how the girl could get an attitude.

At the time, he'd thought about the case so much that he'd gotten headaches. Could her disappearance have had something to do with her role in the courtroom drawings? Nope, that was a stretch, but there were a lot of weirdos out there, and you couldn't rule out anything. What about some of those strange artsy types from Denver that she hung out with occasionally— people who drifted from one art scene to the next? They'd been checked out, too. All claimed to be as mystified as anyone else.

It didn't help that Callie disappeared when she did. Just the day before, he'd turned in his notice that he was leaving for a position on the Denver Police Department. He had only two weeks to work the case. He'd stayed on it twenty hours a day. They'd brought out dogs and search teams, but for all their trouble, there hadn't been one productive lead. Drake sat up again. There was something about the dark, wee hours of the morning that opened the doors to the haunted places in a man's soul. One of his was his failure to find Callie Murphy.

He was waiting for Hadley in the hospital lobby just like he said he would. He was holding Nicky with an assurance he didn't have before, as if he were getting the hang of it. Neither of them looked too much worse for the wear—Drake, lean and even handsomer than she remembered. Nicky's eyes were alight and his arms lifted at the sight of her.

Since she was being forced to remain in the requisite hospital wheelchair until she got into the car, he came over and carefully placed the baby in her lap. Immediately, she showered him with hugs and kisses.

"Do I get one of those, too?" he asked.

She gave him a chiding look. "Not after what I heard about you."

He lifted a perfectly shaped eyebrow, but said nothing. Instead he picked up Nicky and loaded him into the back seat. It was then that she noticed that there was a swatch of something soft and yellow stuck to the back of his overalls. "Drake, wait," she said, reaching up and peeling it off. "What is this?"

He studied it with distaste. "I'd say that was pizza. That was his dessert last night."

She blinked. "And what's that on the front of your shirt?"

"That was the main course, chicken and noodles."

She winced inwardly. He'd had a time of it after all.

He helped her onto the front seat, his touch sure and practiced. What he didn't know about babies, he knew about women. She could tell by the smooth self-assurance with which he touched a shoulder or cupped an elbow. Pushing a woman's buttons, whether consciously or subconsciously, was second nature to him.

"How about a condition report on yourself?" he asked, pulling away from the half-circle drive in front of the hospital. "How do you feel? What did the doctor say?"

"I'm fine," she returned with a smile. "She said I'm healing nicely."

"You'll need help with the baby after you get home." His tone was protective, a mild affront to the independence she'd so carefully cultivated.

"No, I'll manage OK," she said quickly.

She detected a hint of stubbornness around his mouth. It was a sensual mouth, firmly set. She glanced into the back seat to avoid dwelling on it and found Nicky looking contentedly out the window.

"So . . . you heard something about me at the hospital," he

said, coming to a stop at a traffic light. He glanced at her, his eyes bright.

"Someone at the nurses' station recognized you. She said you posed for a police calendar some years ago."

He stroked his jaw, and then looked at her somewhat apologetically. "I was young."

"What were you wearing—or not wearing?"

He kept his eyes on the road but she saw a dimple flash in his cheek. "Spandex shorts with a police logo on the leg."

"Is that all?"

He glanced at her briefly. She detected a smile in his eyes. "Shoes, maybe. They had me posed in front of my bicycle."

Hadley envisioned his chest, tanned, broad and bare, and then took a deep breath to clear her mind. "I hope it was for a good cause."

"As a matter of fact, it was. We raised money for a crime prevention program. Unfortunately, I got more attention from it than I wanted."

"How was that?"

He raked a hand through his hair. "Look, I'm kind of embarrassed about this. To make a long story short, I got a few proposals, one on a billboard, even. I'm already married—to my job—and that's the way I want it. I don't need to tell you the dangers of this line of work."

She twisted her hands in her lap. "No, you don't. Nicky's father was a policeman."

His expression darkened. "I saw the picture in your wallet. I'm truly sorry."

"Thank you."

An awkward silence followed as he turned onto Aspen Street and into Hadley's driveway. He brought the Jeep to a stop and helped her out before unfastening the baby. He kept a protective hand at her elbow until they were on the porch.

Now that she was home, getting this very attractive cop out of the house was at the top of her priority list. Not only did his touch stir something inside her, but he was a walking, talking reminder of how someone you love could be taken away from you in an instant.

He pushed open the door. "Here it is, just like you left it."

Hadley blinked. It wasn't quite. It seemed that every toy Nicky owned was scattered over the living room floor. What appeared to be several small pieces of pizza were trampled into the rug. Wobbly streaks of red crayon marked a wall.

"How did it go?" she asked, though the question was obviously unnecessary.

"Great," he said nonchalantly.

Carefully, she stepped over a stuffed dog and a miniature soccer ball. She was afraid to look in the other rooms.

"I'll straighten up a bit before I leave," he offered. "In the meantime, rest and get your strength back."

She sat gingerly on the sofa. He placed Nicky next to her. It was then that she noticed his overalls were wet. "Drake, I think he needs to be changed."

She rose to do the job herself, but he clamped his hands on her shoulders to prevent her from getting up. He stood the baby on the floor and ripped open the snaps inside the legs. Then he pulled the overalls over the boy's head and tossed them over his shoulder.

Hadley watched his unorthodox changing method with interest. But the biggest curiosity was what the baby wore underneath. Instead of a diaper, it was a red bandanna. Over it was a grocery store produce bag with two holes cut for his legs. It was fastened on each side by a twist tie. She clapped a hand over her mouth to stifle a burst of laughter.

Drake's chin took on a hard set. "Rats, I knew there was something important I forgot. I was going to pick up diapers on the way back from the hospital."

"Are you sure you don't want to apply for a patent on that?" she asked.

"Well, it worked, didn't it?"

She shrugged. "To some degree."

Looking somewhat mollified, he strode toward the door. "Sit tight. I'm going to the store. I'll be right back."

After he left, an unsettling stillness filled the room. It occurred to her that he'd been the first man in the house since the movers and he'd left the biggest impression of all. Not only had he left a mess, but he'd left something percolating inside her, something she hadn't felt in a long time. She could feel it in her veins—warm and effervescent. It was pure chemistry and it needed to be neutralized.

She inched her way into the kitchen to gather more evidence that he was a household hazard and needed to be disposed of as soon as possible. She was almost disappointed to find it in passable order except for the sprinkles of cereal on the counter and a splotch or two of mashed banana. It appeared Nicky had, despite everything, gotten a decent breakfast.

The bedroom was a different story. Her bed was yet unmade, the sheets a tangle, the impression of Drake's head still in the pillow. She looked at it uneasily, her heart producing a little backbeat. Nicky toddled around her with "fresh produce" stamped across his bottom.

In the bathroom was a curious sight—a pair of wet overalls hanging from the showerhead by one strap. Before she could finish her damage assessment survey, she heard the lock turn in the front door. Drake was back with a box of diapers under one arm.

"Heavy duty, leak resistant. That's what the box says. Sounds like a sales pitch for roof shingles."

"Thank you so much." She noticed they were for girls, but

she didn't have the heart to send him back to the store. That would keep him around a little longer and she didn't want that. "Let me pay you back for everything."

"Your wallet and personal things, incidentally, are still locked up at the station. So is your car. We'll work out the details later."

"You've done too much already," she protested. Then, without thinking and out of sheer force of habit, she reached down and picked up Nicky. A splitting pain shot through her side. She barely managed to put him down without dropping him.

Drake slipped his arms around her and helped her back to the sofa.

"Let me see if you've broken any stitches," he said. She winced as he gently lifted the red sweater she had worn into and out of the hospital. He pulled up a corner of the bandage just above the waistband of her jeans. She turned away, afraid to look. His breath flickered against her skin.

"Still intact," he said.

She sighed in relief.

He patted the bandage back into place, pulled down her sweater, and then faced her squarely. "Hadley, you shouldn't be trying to manage by yourself."

She sat up, pretending it no longer hurt. "I'll be fine. I'll just have to be careful."

"Look," he said firmly, "Nicky weighs a good thirty pounds and you can't avoid lifting him. I'll stick around a couple of days until you get on your feet."

Her stomach tightened. "No, I can't let you."

His gaze was direct and left no room for argument. "I'm not going to let you put yourself at risk. Case closed."

Chapter Three

Before she could come back with a rebuttal, the sound of shattering glass exploded from the kitchen. It was followed by a wail.

"Nicky!" She leapt halfway to her feet.

Drake's hand went to her shoulder before she could stand up. Then with the quickness and grace of a panther, he was off and running.

"What is it?" she yelled, getting up to follow him. She was barely a step away from the sofa before he was back, the toddler draped over his arm like a towel.

Drake shot her a look of disapproval when he saw her standing. "Just what do you think you're doing?"

"I'm checking on my son."

"Your son is fine, just a little surprised, that's all. He pulled a cereal bowl off the counter."

Realizing she'd forgotten to tell Drake to use Nicky's plastic dinnerware, she automatically reached out to take the whimpering toddler into her arms.

He held the boy away from her. "Please, sit down. If you want to do something for Nicky, rest and recuperate. I'm here to help. I thought we'd already settled that."

She took a deep breath. She was grateful for this offer of assistance from a virtual stranger, a tall and gallant one at that. But she didn't want to become friends with a man who could be plucked out of her life in an instant. Yet right now, there was no one else and for Nicky's sake, she had to accept his help.

She leaned back against the sofa, finally conceding he was right. "Well, now you know," she said. "He's like a little octopus with tentacles grabbing in all directions."

Drake offered a stiff nod. "Octopus twins."

With Nicky beside her on the sofa, she listened to the rhythm of Drake's steps as he swept the broken china off the kitchen floor. Even though he was outside her range of vision, his presence was a powerful one, one that went straight to her core where past hurts and fears were hidden.

Hadley heard a few mysterious bangs and clatters, then the sound of water running. Some minutes later, he reappeared. "How about some lunch?" he asked brightly.

She sat up. "You do lunch, too?"

"Sure. You have a can opener, don't you?"

Hadley pursed her lips to keep from smiling. "In the drawer by the sink. There's soup in the pantry. I usually feed Nicky first, then I put him down for his nap."

"I'll take care of lunch for everybody," he said.

A short time later, he reappeared, announcing, "Soup's on for Nicky."

"I'll feed him," Hadley insisted. Sore though she might be, she was anxious to be a hands-on mommy again.

Drake picked up the baby and offered Hadley a helping hand. Grudgingly, she took it. The heat of his touch lingered as she walked carefully beside him.

In the kitchen, she watched as he strapped Nicky in his high chair and set a bowl of stew in front of him. Next to the bowl he laid a wet washcloth, as if he'd learned a thing or two while she was gone.

She eased into a chair next to the boy. Making airplane noises, she began maneuvering spoons of food into his mouth.

Suddenly, she became conscious of being watched. She

turned to find Drake leaning against the doorjamb, his arms folded across his chest. The barest of smiles caused a corner of his mouth to crinkle upward.

Hadley set down the spoon. "You must think I've lost it."

He strolled toward her. "Actually, I think you've got everything together. You're a wonder, even."

Her eyes caught the gray depths of his and for an instant time seemed to stop. She felt the color in her cheeks deepen.

"I admire your strength, Hadley. I know things haven't been easy."

She feigned nonchalance. "When you have a child, you're strong for his sake. If you're not strong, you pretend."

"You're not pretending."

She avoided Drake's eyes. They stirred feelings in her, feelings that she didn't want to feel anymore. She wiped the boy's face with the washcloth and kissed his forehead. She looked up to find Drake's gaze still on her.

"Why are you going to so much trouble for Nicky and me?"

"Cops look out for each other and each other's families," he said flatly.

"Don't you think you might want a family of your own someday?"

He shook his head firmly. "I made up my mind about that a long time ago." He looked at the baby, then back at Hadley, rendering further explanation unnecessary.

"I understand why you might feel that way," she said softly.

Suddenly, an acrid smell rolled through the kitchen, followed by a hissing sound. Drake dashed toward the stove.

He muttered something unintelligible, then held up a charred and smoking saucepan. Color tinged his cheeks. "The soup burned."

Hadley slapped a hand over her mouth to hide her smile, but she was too late.

"Don't laugh. It was your last can," he grumbled.

"A sandwich would be fine," she said. "I'll take peanut butter and jelly."

After lunch, if one could call it that, Drake set off again for the grocery store. He had to get out of Hadley Spencer's house for a while. It wasn't just a house, it was a home. There were toys, windows filled with sunshine, and baby laughter. Then there was Hadley herself, fresh and wide-eyed. She was making him have certain thoughts, and he could tell that she wasn't even trying. He knew when a woman was trying. It didn't take a detective to pick up those clues.

In fact, if she had much of a choice, she probably would have sent him packing by now, he figured. She tolerated him only because there was no one else. It wasn't because he was a man. It wasn't because he could protect her. And it certainly wasn't because of his cooking.

She'd grown accustomed to managing alone and he sensed a pride in that independence. She'd think twice before giving up her heart again—if she gave it up at all. That's what his instincts told him. He trusted the feelings that dwelled deep in his gut. Those instincts had kept him alive on several occasions.

She'd asked straight out why he was doing so much for her and the baby. That was a question he'd been asking himself. He didn't have to do some of the little things like tightening the loose screw on the handle on the silverware drawer, or taking out the garbage when there was hardly any to take out. Why he was going beyond the call of duty was something he wasn't particularly anxious to explore.

This whole business with Hadley Spencer disturbed him on two different levels: It stirred up painful memories of his own losses and it put him in the shoes of a fallen comrade. It all went to show that the wall he'd built around his heart wasn't impenetrable after all.

He parked the Jeep in front of the grocery store and glanced at the short list that Hadley had given him. Angel hair pasta. Dijon mustard. Why did women do this? Why not buy a few cans of beans and wieners and let it go at that? They had to take something simple like food and get artsy with it. Just about the only things on the list that made any sense were milk and Spaghetti-O's.

He grabbed a small basket and wandered down the pasta aisle.

"Hi, Drake," someone said.

He turned to the sound of the lilting feminine voice behind him. It was his commander's daughter, who was undoubtedly Mountain Spring's sexiest kindergarten teacher. Being nearly as tall as he, she beamed a florescent smile right at him. It seemed she'd had a knack lately for popping up at the station just as he got off work. Now, he was on her turf. He hoped she didn't read anything into that.

"Hi, Mitzi. What a surprise."

"Isn't it, though?" She wore jeans and a snug black top with a dipping neckline that showcased her ample curves. Her dark hair was caught in a pert ponytail and her lips were lacquered a candy-apple red. "Dad said you were going to spend some time on the Killarney. Unless they moved it, the river is about a hundred miles from here."

"Right you are—on both counts."

"You're not cheating and buying your fish at the grocery store, are you?" she asked coyly.

"No, I'm just visiting a friend for a few days," he said with amusement, "and then I'll be on my way."

She cocked her head coquettishly. "I was going to call you when you got back. But since we're both here, I might as well ask you now."

"Ask away." His tone was light, but inwardly, he braced himself. The last time he'd spoken to grade school kids he'd caught some kind of stomach virus that was going around. It had taken him out of commission for two days.

"I thought it would be nice if we could go to the police hoedown together," she said. "Dad says it's loads of fun. And it's for a good cause."

Drake blinked. Hal Benson was his former partner and a terrific guy. But he was now his superior officer. No, this was getting too complicated.

"Mitzi," he said, "I'm sorry, but I already have a date."

Her eyes dulled with disappointment. "Well, maybe we can go out some other time."

"Maybe." Lie number two.

She smiled as if "maybe" meant "yes," and then with a quick wave, she flounced off toward the dairy case.

Drake felt like someone had just snatched his gun from his holster. *I already have a date,* he repeated silently, mocking himself. He'd actually lied. How had he let that happen? Cops didn't lie. Well, one thing was for certain. He was going to have to show up at that hoedown or his absence was going to be duly noted by his old buddy—and commander.

With help from several stock boys, he managed to find all of Hadley's exotic goodies. Hearts of palm. Good grief. It was wonderful not being married, and having to deal with this every day.

Driving home, he pondered the tight spot he'd gotten himself into with Mitzi. She'd taken him down like a sitting duck. There had been a time when it had all been part of a game to which he had been a very willing player. But he'd grown increasingly tired of it. The challenge was gone and it seemed increasingly pointless. After all, he wasn't looking for Ms. Right.

Ultimately, commitment was what women were after. They

wanted love, a home, and babies. That was something he couldn't—wouldn't—give.

Hadley looked down at the pallet on which Nicky was sleeping on the bedroom floor. His small chest rose and fell in a sweet and steady rhythm. Drake had made the makeshift cot so she wouldn't have to lift him in and out of his crib.

But sleep had eluded her. She stared at the ceiling as his voice echoed in her ears.

He had bathed Nicky, leaving the bathroom looking as if it lay in the wake of a thrashing thunderstorm. Water and towels were everywhere. On the bed, he'd left his scent—the faint tang of cedar freshly cut in the crisp, clear air of winter.

He couldn't cook, he knew next to nothing about babies, and he'd posed for a beefcake calendar. This was not the sort of man who would boldly step in to take control in a domestic crisis. This was not the sort of man one would want to step in. But he did, and therein laid the paradox. Somewhere deep inside that powerful form, with muscles worked into steel, was a soft, liquid center.

She knew what police work did to men. It forced them to put up guards, to blunt their feelings, to grow emotional calluses. The hardening process in Drake Matthieson was well advanced but something kept him from turning completely to flint. She'd seen it in his eyes as he'd sat and watched her feed the baby.

Despite his somewhat glaring shortcomings as a maid, nanny and nurse, Hadley found herself missing him. And that frightened her. The sooner he was gone for good, the better.

After what seemed to be an inordinately long time for a trip to the grocery store, Hadley heard the front door open. Carefully, she got up. Still wearing her oversized red sweater, jeans and woolen socks, she shuffled into the living room to greet him.

Carrying a paper bag in each arm, he pushed the door shut with his heel. "You're supposed to be in bed," he said.

"You're supposed to say 'hello' first."

He wrinkled his nose at her. "You're feeling better, I see."

"I'll help you put away the groceries, even." The sooner she could convince him that she could manage on her own, the better. He looked down at her with those unreadable smoke gray eyes and shook his head slowly. "No lifting. Not even a can of palms of hearts."

"Hearts of palm," she corrected, noticing he smelled of evergreen.

"I didn't realize palms had hearts." He paused and then looked at her warily. "You don't feed them to Nicky, do you?"

"No. I was thinking about feeding them to you."

He lifted an eyebrow.

"They're a delicacy," she explained. "They go in a special chicken recipe. We're having it for supper."

Without saying anything, he strode into the kitchen and set the bags on the counter with a thump. Hadley was several paces behind him.

He paused in the kitchen doorway, blocking her entry. Leveling his gaze at her, he traced a finger over her shoulder then let his hand drop.

Her blood puddled around her heart.

"Hadley, you're not getting the message. You're not in any shape to be whipping up a gourmet meal."

"I owe you," she argued. "It's the least I can do. It will be no trouble at all. I even promise to let you lift it out of the oven."

Suddenly, Nicky toddled into the kitchen, rubbing his eyes.

The sight of him warmed her and she pulled him close. "So much for needing Mommy anymore. Without the crib, he does well enough on his own."

"That was the idea," Drake said.

Hadley took a two-handled cup from the refrigerator and handed it to Nicky.

"Back to supper," Drake said. "Don't think I don't appreciate what you're trying to do, but tonight, I'm in charge. And I brought supper—Chinese. It's still in the car. The guy there gives me extra."

Hadley stepped back from the door. For being willing to lay down their lives in the pursuit of justice, cops got extra egg rolls and free cups of coffee, maybe a doughnut or a wave. Her heart constricted. The offering seemed so small for a sacrifice that could be so large.

Drake went back outside for the Chinese food, and set it on the kitchen counter.

"If you want to do something to please me, get some more rest before dinner," he said. "In the meantime, I'll take Nicky for a stroll."

She'd barely had time to protest before he stepped out on the porch, planted the boy in his stroller, and wheeled him down the sidewalk.

Pouring herself a glass of milk, Hadley caught a glimpse of them from the kitchen window as they disappeared down the tree-lined street. Drake's long legs moved with the halting steps of a man unaccustomed to such domestic pursuits. She shook her head at the absurdity of the scene. Her innocent baby was being wheeled around by a certified ladies' man, a gun-toting one at that. At least he'd left his service revolver somewhere else.

That aside, there they were together—a man and a baby. That's the way she had pictured the future. But the man in the snapshots of her mind had been Quint. So much for pictures; so much for plans. Someday, Nicky would have a father. He just wouldn't be a man who might be called upon to give the ultimate sacrifice.

In preparation for their return, she set out some items for the baby's supper. Then suddenly a cloud of fatigue descended over her, catching her by surprise. Opening a few cabinet doors couldn't have done it. Dealing with Drake Matthieson's very masculine presence could have. She walked painstakingly back into the living room and sank into the sofa.

Before she could re-charge herself, they were back. Nicky's cheeks were rosy from the brisk spring air. Drake's restless energy seemed yet unspent. This was a man, she guessed, who was unaccustomed to spending a lot of time indoors.

"We saw a cat, two squirrels, and a woman in Spandex," he said. "I thought you might want a report."

Hadley thought of the Barbie-like jogger down the street, the brunette who was two-thirds legs. He was a bachelor. Why shouldn't he look? Just the same, she felt a vague and disturbing twinge of disappointment.

"Thank you. I trust you didn't burn the tires off my son's stroller chasing after her."

"In my younger days, I might have."

"Of course, it might be hard to pick up girls with a baby in tow," she observed.

"Who knows?" he shrugged. "Babies could make good lures."

Hadley gave him a threatening look in case he might be contemplating using her son for such a scheme, and then eased herself up off the sofa.

Drake nudged her back down. "Let's not overdo it. I'll feed Nicky this time."

Nicky's supper took a good half hour, counting the time to clean up the mess afterwards. With chicken potpie in his ear and applesauce in his hair, the toddler needed another bath. Then the bathroom had to be wiped up and the towels washed, including the ones Drake had neglected to pick up after Nicky's previous bath. One job led to another.

48

"How do you do it all by yourself?" he asked, once the boy had been put to bed.

"You just do it, and then you get better at it," she said simply.

"Now, I'll get down to the part I'm better at." He inspected her small collection of compact disks and selected an orchestral rendition of a series of old rock songs. He stuck it in the CD player. He switched off a lamp, leaving a lone one to cast a dim golden glow over the room.

"What are you doing?" Hadley asked suspiciously.

"I'm just providing a little atmosphere."

"Atmosphere for what?"

A playful twitch appeared at the corner of his mouth. So far, that seemed to be the closest he could get to a smile. "The answer to that varies from place to place," he said.

Forgetting her incision, she put her hands on her hips. "Ouch," she said, her right hand flying out from her side. "You'd better be just trying to conserve electricity."

"I'm trying to provide a relaxing atmosphere, to pamper you a little," he said. "You deserve it."

She gave him a grudging look. After the ordeal of the past few days, she could use it. But when Drake Matthieson's definition of "pampering" seemed to include soft music and low lights, an internal alarm went off.

"As the pamperee, I have a suggestion," she said. "We can have a nice supper, then you can go home and rest up for work on Monday."

"I'm not going to work."

She blinked. "What do you mean? Don't you have to be on duty?"

He shook his head. "Remember? You conveniently had your emergency appendectomy just as my vacation was beginning."

Her gut tightened, making her stitches pull. "Now, I do. I feel terrible. You had other plans. I probably ruined them."

He offered a shrug. "A few days won't make any difference. The fish will still be biting."

"I'm really grateful for all you've done," she said.

"Don't mention it." He stepped into the dining room and lit the two candles on the table. Then, he produced a bouquet of mixed flowers from the refrigerator. Hadley watched with growing trepidation. "Why flowers? And candles?" Her voice, normally sure and steady, cracked.

"Ask yourself. They're your candles. As for the flowers, they were on sale. Besides, I didn't bring you any when you were in the hospital."

That reminded her that nobody did because she hardly knew anyone except her aunt and her business clients. At this moment, Drake was all she had, a fact that didn't entirely please her. "Thank you. You're very thoughtful."

He offered one of his little near-smiles, and then went about warming up the cartons of Chinese food in the microwave. His body moved with the ease and fluidity of a finely tuned machine.

He'd chosen three dishes, one spicy, one sweet, and one savory, and they ate as the candles flickered between them. The light played over the strong angles of his jaw, gilding his skin.

"What led you into police work?" she asked, somewhat awkwardly.

"An accident," he said after a short pause. "It killed my immediate family—all except me."

Hadley's stomach clutched and she laid down her fork. "How tragic." Her voice dwindled to a whisper. "If you'd rather not talk about it . . ."

"No, it's OK" He paused for a moment as if to get his bearings. "My father was crowded off the road by a drunk driver. The car went down an embankment. Both of my parents died along with a younger brother and sister. I was the only one who survived. I was thirteen." He touched his chin. "That's where this scar came from."

Her heart twisted. "I'm so sorry."

He continued, his face expressionless. "A state trooper investigating the accident spent a lot of time with me since I was the only witness. He kept on the case for a year. That's how long it took to nail the suspect. I came to have a lot of respect for the trooper and his work. That's the story."

A heavy silence filled the room.

"You haven't said much about Nicky's father," he ventured.

She took a deep breath. "He was killed by a burglary suspect. He was even wearing a bullet-proof vest."

Drake reached across the table and placed his hand over hers, sending a wave of heat rolling toward her heart. "You don't need to say any more."

But she did, suddenly feeling a need. "I found out a month later that I was pregnant with Nicky."

Drake blinked.

"Now, Nicky is pretty much my life."

"That's easy to see."

"I knew the risks of marrying a cop, but somehow, you don't think those things you hear about will happen to you."

"Fortunately, they don't happen often. But they do happen. And in my case . . . Well, it doesn't help that I head up a SWAT team. Add that to what I went through as a kid and you can see why I feel more comfortable staying single. It keeps things simple."

She smiled ruefully. "I think we understand each other perfectly."

His gray gaze took on added depth. "If you ever need me, Hadley, I'll be here—as a friend. I've got a good ear for listening and a shoulder to cry on."

Her heart gave a little yank. She couldn't afford to need him, to even imagine that she could feel safe with him. If anything, he was a threat to the neat, orderly and predictable independence she'd created for herself.

She pulled her hand away from his. "Thank you. But I don't know how I can repay you as it is. You may have literally saved my life. There must be something I can do."

He looked at her contemplatively. A playful flicker appeared in his eyes. "Well, come to think of it, there might be."

CHAPTER FOUR

The flicker in his eyes had just enough of the devil in it to put her on guard. "What is it?"

"Would you pretend to be my date for a dance?"

Hadley's breath stalled in her chest.

His expression turned serious. "I wouldn't ask, except that I'm in sort of an awkward situation."

"What do you mean?" she asked warily.

"While I was at the grocery store earlier, I ran into the daughter of my ex-partner, who is now my division commander. She invited me to the police hoedown. It's a fund-raiser for the crime watch program. I told her I already had a date."

"What happened? Did your date cancel?"

He rubbed his jaw. "No. The truth is I had to do something I almost never do. I lied. Mitzi's one of those women used to getting what she wants. In this case, it happens to be me. She's also the apple of her father's eye. He doesn't want anybody disappointing his little girl without good reason. Dating the boss's daughter? Nope, I'm not setting foot on that rickety bridge."

"I see what you mean. But why me?" Hadley asked. "Don't you have a little black book or something?"

A touch of mirth appeared on his lips. "It's red, actually. But to be honest, I'm sitting out the game these days. I'm thirty-six years old and I'm through leading women on a merry chase. With you, I don't have to worry. I'm not after you and you're not after me. In fact, I'm sure the last guy you'd want to get involved with is a cop. And for all I know, you don't even like me that much." He looked at her questioningly, with one neatly angled brow lifted in an unspoken plea. "I'd appreciate it if you could help me out, though. As I said, it wouldn't be a real date."

Hadley, perusing her options, none of them good, gnawed for a moment on her bottom lip.

"I mean—It's not that I don't find you attractive," he continued. "You definitely are, but that's beside the point. This would just be a matter of one person returning another person's favor, nothing more."

"Sort of like the barter system?" she asked.

"Yeah, or like an Amish barn-raising."

She sighed. It had been three years since Quint's death and she still had no desire to go out. In time, it would come, but the time was not now. Her heart and her instincts, which had served her reasonably well in the past, would let her know when.

In the meantime, this Mitzi-evasion strategy that Drake had proposed sounded benign enough. It was a deal and not a date. He'd made that clear. After all he'd done for her, how could she refuse? There was no need to worry about his getting any ideas because he'd all but said that she wasn't his type. What his type was, she didn't exactly know, but she imagined Spandex-clad fitness enthusiasts with bouncing ponytails.

"When is it?" she asked finally.

His eyes brightened. "Three weeks from Saturday. I'll even pay for a baby-sitter—the best we can find. Cost is no object."

"Mitzi's that tenacious?"

He nodded gravely.

Hadley thought of how she had ruined the first few days of Drake's vacation and her guilt deepened. "All right. I'll go, as long as it's not a real date."

"Thanks, Hadley. You're a real pal." He raised a hand in a

high-five gesture.

Clumsily, she slapped her palm against his. It was as steady as a boulder. Its heat traveled to her heart with lightning speed.

"I'll pick you up at eight," he said, without missing a beat. "And tomorrow, I'll be back to help out."

Hadley shook her head adamantly. "That's very nice of you, Drake, but Aunt Margaret is due back in town tomorrow night. She loves Nicky and would be very disappointed not to be needed."

"You're sure? She'll probably be tired from her trip."

"Not Aunt Margaret. She jogs two miles a day; has since she was fifty."

Drake's eyes narrowed slightly. "Fifty? How old is she now?"

"A very young seventy."

He blinked.

"She can drive me to have my stitches taken out and do any lifting that I can't do. You should see her with her three-pound weights. She can practically juggle them."

His expression remained skeptical.

Well, maybe that was a bit of an exaggeration, but, despite his kindness, she still wanted him out of the house. His voice was too rich and full. His mouth was too sensuous. All said, he was an attractive nuisance.

"Please, Drake, promise me that you'll leave on your vacation tomorrow," she urged. "I'll feel terrible if you don't."

"All right," he quickly agreed.

She looked at him in mild surprise. She was expecting more resistance.

"That is, if you're sure you don't need me," he added.

"I'm positive."

"Then I'll leave you in the care of Superaunt." He took his napkin from his lap, laid it beside his empty plate and started to rise. "It's getting late and I really should be going."

Her heart reacted with an inexplicable thud. "What about your fortune cookie?" She nudged a Blue Willow salad plate closer to him. Strips of paper peeped from two golden-brown crescents.

His mouth took on a skeptical slant. He took one and sat back down. Hadley became aware that the music, barely audible, was still playing, adding an unwanted feeling of intimacy to the room. After so many dozens of women, she figured, candles and music were probably standard operating procedure for Drake Matthieson. They were a habit to which he hardly gave a thought.

He snapped open the cookie and pulled out the ribbon of paper inside. "Ginger is the spice of life," he read. A short pause followed. "Funny, there was a Ginger in my life once and that's exactly what I thought at the time. We were in kindergarten and, for Valentine's Day, I gave her a red cloth heart. The problem was that I'd snipped it out of one of my grandmother's heirloom quilts. While Ginger was pleased, it wasn't a good Valentine's Day for Grandma."

Hadley laughed, and then shook her head disapprovingly. She imagined Drake as a handsome, sturdy boy, full of exuberance for life and unafraid to bare his feelings. What a contrast to the man who now lived within disciplined bounds, who wanted to be close to no one.

"What are you going to do when Nicky does something like that?" he asked. The light from a small stained-glass lamp on the buffet played over his smile.

"To start with, I can't imagine Nicky as a kindergarten Romeo," she said.

He shrugged. "Boys will be boys."

"Not Nicky, not like that."

"Maybe not, but there will be other adventures. Take it from a former boy. But there's nothing to worry about. Most of us turn out just fine. Look at me. I'm not so bad, am I?" There was a teasing glint in his eyes.

She smiled and shook her head, but a feeling of sadness quickly followed. She wished she could be both mother and father to her son, but she knew better. It would be nice if he had a father, someone who could guide him through the ups and downs of boyhood, someone who was kind, considerate of others and who would be a good role model by making a meaningful contribution to society. Then, she realized, with a twist of anxiety, that she had just described Drake.

"What's wrong?" he asked. "You look as if you just swallowed a bug."

"Nothing," she fibbed.

He reached over and lightly touched her wrist with his finger. "You haven't opened your cookie."

Hadley was momentarily distracted by his touch. It made her pulse race.

He inched the plate toward her.

She removed the twist of paper and smoothed it with her fingers. "Get in touch with your inner child."

Drake took it and examined it. Then he looked up at her for what seemed to be a few very long seconds. His gaze was clear and searching. Hadley's heart skipped.

"Have you ever done anything daring or adventurous?"

"Not that I can remember."

"Rash or impulsive?"

"Of course not."

"Anything just for fun whether it made any sense or not?"

"Can't think of anything."

"That's what I figured," he said.

Hadley eyed him warily. "What do you mean?"

"You're a play-it-safe kind of woman. On that day you came weaving up to the station, I almost never got Nicky out of that maximum-security child seat."

"I guess I've gotten a little obsessive since Quint died." A weighty stillness fell over her.

Drake's eyes turned as dark as a starless night. "I'm sorry. I didn't mean to . . ."

"It's all right. Really, it is. I've gotten past a lot of it."

"Then maybe you should give the fortune cookie advice some serious thought. Wade in puddles after a rain. Have ice cream for supper if you feel like it. Life is short, and you just never know."

Hadley's gaze locked onto his in mutual understanding. They'd both suffered losses—he even more than she. But that sort of child-like exuberance for life was no longer within her, and Hadley wasn't sure it could ever be again.

"Throw caution to the wind and life could be even shorter," she countered.

He leaned back in his chair and folded his arms across his chest. "And less fun. How are you going to know which is best unless you try them both?"

"You're impossible."

A twinkle appeared in his eyes. "That's what my grandmother used to say."

"What did your grandmother say when you performed surgery on her quilt?"

"Plenty. I spent the next day weeding her flower beds while she mended it."

Hadley laughed softly. "She sounds like a wise woman."

"Was," he corrected gently. "She died just a few years later."

She cast him a look of sympathy.

"The funny thing was that I think she grew to like that quilt even more because of that patch," he said.

"I bet she did."

An awkward silence followed. His chin crinkled, Drake stared at the oak tabletop as if his thoughts had taken him to a universe away from Hadley's little gray bungalow. Abruptly, he rose.

"It's time for me to go."

She stood across from him, slightly startled by his sudden change of tone. The emotional guard that he'd let down ever so slightly seemed to snap firmly back into place. "Drake, thanks for everything. I would have had a hard time managing without you."

A slight smile touched his lips, but it seemed to come with effort. "That's part of my job—to serve. I'm glad I was able to help."

She walked with him to the front door. Even out of uniform, he had a presence so large that he seemed to fill her small living room all by himself.

He placed a hand on the doorknob, and then turned toward her. "Thanks for agreeing to help with the Mitzi problem. You're a real sport."

"It's the least I could do," she said.

He reached out and cuffed her lightly on the arm as if she were a teammate. "I'm glad you understand."

She nodded, her arm tingling.

He stepped through the door and disappeared into the night. Careful not to overdo it, Hadley threw herself into tidying up the kitchen. But no amount of busywork could distract her from the vacuum he'd left behind.

Drake switched on the light in his second-floor apartment, illuminating a worn, but serviceable, brown tweed sofa and bare, white walls. Dozens of back issues of professional journals were stacked in no particular order on the carpet next to his one indulgence—a brown leather club chair with a matching ottoman. The whole setup had looked perfectly fine before, had been welcoming even after a pressure-filled day, but now it didn't seem quite the same. He thought of Hadley's polished oak floors and sage green walls filled with gold-framed watercolors. Then there were the needlework pillows that seemed to reach out to embrace a man's tired muscles. After two days of such hominess, his own place had all the ambiance of a one-star motel.

It smelled of dust and stale pepperoni, he realized for the first time. Hers smelled of baby powder, citrus and spice. A man could actually learn to like coming home to a place like that.

Thank goodness that senior fitness queen of an aunt was due back in town soon. Thank goodness he could finally make his escape to the Killarney. No hearts of palm for him. He was a meat and potatoes man. No diaper-changing for him, either, although the kid kind of grew on him, sort of like a puppy.

Most of all, he needed to get away from her and those dark-lashed pale-blue eyes. Once, they'd made him lose his train of thought. He couldn't have that. Well, they'd made a deal, and when the hoedown was over, both of them could go back to their respective lives. End of story.

He strolled into the bedroom and set his alarm for 5 a.m. He'd be at the Killarney by eight, just in time to see the morning sun filter through the forest, turning it emerald green. And with any luck, he'd have a nice trout for supper, cooked over a wood fire.

He was contemplating the succulence of a five-pounder when the phone rang. He looked at his watch. It was almost eleven. His adrenaline kicked in, putting him in a state of readiness, as he grabbed the receiver from the nightstand.

"Drake Matthieson."

"Drake, it's Hadley." Her voice had an undertone of concern to it.

His gut tightened. "Anything wrong?"

"Yes, and no. Aunt Margaret's tour company called. She

won't be back tonight after all. Something is wrong with their tour bus and they're waiting for a replacement. They don't expect to arrive in Denver until tomorrow afternoon. The problem is that I'm supposed to be at the Mountain Spring Medical Clinic at 8:30 tomorrow morning for a follow-up exam and I'm still not supposed to drive."

His shoulders sagged.

"Would you mind?" Her voice had a touch of pride in it as if she didn't like having to ask. "I hate to bother you, after all you've done. I should be out by 9:30. You weren't planning to leave on your trip too terribly early, were you?"

"No," he fibbed. "I'll take you. How does eight-fifteen sound?"

"Fine. Thank you, Drake. Good night."

"Night." He hung up and let out a very long sigh. How could he have said no? But what bothered him most, was part of him had wanted very much to say yes.

Hadley hadn't slept well the night before. She'd awakened with her pillow flung halfway across the room and a sheet tangled around her ankle. She'd hated calling Drake, but Mountain Spring had no taxi service and the baby-sitter still hadn't returned. She'd thought better of asking Mr. Knickerbocker who lived next door. His new Buick already sported a collection of dents and scrapes and just recently, he'd returned from the senior citizens center with a crumpled front fender. Postponing her appointment wasn't practical because the doctor was leaving for a medical convention the following afternoon. That left Drake.

She was awake before the alarm went off. Not up to her usual speed, it took her a half hour longer than usual to get Nicky ready. Once he was fed, she dressed him in blue denim overalls and a red long-sleeved t-shirt. She had just managed to toss on a blue knit pants set, and apply a smudge of lipstick when the doorbell rang.

She found Drake standing on the porch with his hands shoved into the pockets of an old pair of dark green military-style cargo pants. They were topped with a frayed gray sweatshirt. "Hi," he said. "Your chariot awaits."

He looked somewhat sleepy-eyed, but very sexy with his glistening shower-dampened hair and skin scrubbed to a glow. Hadley glanced over his shoulder, trying not to spend a second longer than necessary looking at him. The "chariot" was loaded with fly rods and camping gear. Before they got in, Drake tossed a few police magazines to the floor to clear a space for Nicky's child safety seat. He seemed to be getting the hang of it now, this art of managing toddler and accompanying paraphernalia. Hadley watched as he strapped the seat into place with the ease of saddling an old mount. There was also something different about the way he handled Nicky. There was a sureness to his motions that wasn't there before, as if he were handling a basketball instead of an egg.

"I feel so bad imposing on you again," Hadley said as he backed out of the driveway. "I really hated to do it, but it was either you or Mr. Knickerbocker."

"Who's Mr. Knickerbocker?"

"My 90-year-old neighbor."

"The one with tire ruts on both sides of his driveway?"

"That's him."

"Wise choice. Promise you'll call me again if it comes down to that."

Hadley hesitated. She'd think of something else before she called either Drake or Mr. Knickerbocker. "I'd rather promise not to bother you again."

He glanced at her. "It's not a bother. We're friends. Friends help each other out."

Hadley gave him a tight-lipped smile. She couldn't argue with his philosophy of friendship. But she would feel more at ease if this self-described "pal" were short, balding and would never think of leaving Mother.

"I hope the fish haven't fled for safer waters."

"So what? Fish aren't the only reason I fish."

"What do you mean? Isn't catching fish the point of fishing?"

"Well, yes, but there are other benefits—like the way nature renews a person's spirit. In my work, that's important. As you well know."

Silence fell between them. She glanced back at Nicky to distract herself from the memories that were pushing their way out of a carefully guarded compartment in her mind. The meals that Quint had missed. The times she'd waited up for him. The night he'd awakened, drenched with sweat from a frightening dream. She turned, gave one of Nicky's sneakers a playful jiggle and smiled at him. He smiled back, and that, she realized, was her own healing balm.

Drake turned and deftly wheeled the Jeep into the clinic parking lot. As soon as he stopped, Hadley got out of the car. Before she could get Nicky out of his seat, Drake was there to make sure she didn't. With ease, he hoisted the boy up and carried him in the bend of his arm.

Hadley quickened her pace. She wanted her doctor's appointment over and her freedom back—freedom from needing someone, especially Drake. Because at this moment, Nicky was grinning from ear to ear as if the man carrying him were Santa Claus.

It was early and they were the only ones in the waiting room. Under Drake's watch, Nicky rummaged through a basket of toys. Hadley thumbed distractedly through a decorating magazine. Suddenly, a door clicked open. An elderly man limped out, followed quickly by a tall redhead in green scrubs.

"Mr. Mendenhall," she called after him, holding up a set of keys. "Are these yours?"

"Oh, mercy me," he said with an embarrassed smile. "Thank you, young lady."

"You're quite welcome."

The woman turned back toward the waiting area, took a few steps, then stopped in her tracks.

"Drake Matthieson, is that you?"

Drake stood up. "Cherie—it's been a long time." His voice had an intimate quality to it, as if their paths had not only crossed but criss-crossed. Hadley could see from her nametag that she was a registered nurse.

Cherie glanced at Hadley. "You're married?"

"No, she's just a friend," he said quickly.

"You could have fooled me. You looked the picture of domestic bliss."

He took in a breath so sharp that Hadley heard it. She turned to find Drake, normally the quintessence of cool reserve, looking somewhat flustered. "You should know better."

Her smile faded. "I guess I should."

Awkwardly, Drake introduced Hadley. Hadley offered her hand. Cherie slipped a tepid palm inside hers, and then quickly withdrew it.

The brief introduction was cut even shorter when the receptionist announced to Hadley that the doctor was ready to see her. Relieved, she excused herself, but only after making sure that Drake's attention was properly focused on Nicky.

Drake had been forthcoming about his past relationships with women, yet she felt vaguely unsettled by his encounter with Cherie—so much so that she hardly noticed when the doctor poked around her incision. What bothered her most was not his reaction to seeing a past girlfriend, but her own reaction to it. Was she actually starting to like having him around?

She shouldn't, because he had plenty of faults. Besides being a ladies' man, he tracked mud in the house. Furthermore, he left drawers open and lights on. She'd have to sit down and make a complete list of his flaws as soon as she got home. Post them on the refrigerator, even.

When she left the examining room, there was no trace of Cherie. Instead, she found Drake with Nicky on his lap and a book in his hand. He was reading "The Poky Puppy." His voice was rich and full of inflection. Nicky, his corn-colored hair appearing even lighter in contrast to Drake's, was so engrossed that Hadley's entrance went unnoticed.

A grandmotherly woman with springy white curls smiled sweetly at her from a chair a few feet away, then looked back at Drake.

Suddenly, he looked up, stopping in mid-sentence. "Whoops." He shut the book with a snap. He looked slightly embarrassed. "How long have you been standing there?"

"What happened to your cop's heightened senses?"

"I'm on vacation, remember?"

Hadley gave him a look of disbelief.

"You certainly make a lovely family," the old woman observed. There was a twinkle of nostalgia in her eyes.

Hadley saw a muscle twitch in Drake's jaw. "He's just a friend," she explained quickly.

The older woman looked slightly puzzled. Hadley sensed there was a lot to modern male-female relationships that probably went beyond her comprehension.

"What did the doctor say?" Drake asked as they left the clinic. Each of them held one of Nicky's hands as he toddled between them.

"She said I'm fine, that I can resume my normal activities as long as I take it easy in the beginning."

"That's good to hear."

Hadley was equally glad to hear it. Her life could get back to normal, life without Drake Matthieson and all his charms.

In the car, Hadley began to breathe easier. She was just a hoedown away from life before Drake.

He started the engine and put the transmission in reverse. But before backing out of the parking space, he glanced at himself in the rearview mirror, studying his face from several angles. He turned to Hadley, looking mildly perplexed.

"I don't look married, do I?"

A gurgle of a laugh escaped from Hadley's throat. "What is 'married' supposed to look like?"

"I don't know—missing that certain sparkle and friskiness."

Hadley listened with amusement. "I thought that was called getting older."

He frowned slightly. "No, that's not it. It's looking like your first choice of a vehicle would be a minivan; your second choice, a riding lawnmower."

"Maybe it's looking content."

His frown deepened, bordering on a scowl.

"Who is Cherie?" she probed.

"She was a girlfriend—once. We met when she was an emergency room nurse and I was working an assault case. We had some great times. But she wanted more—you know, all the things that women want."

There he was, talking to her again like a pal. Like they might go out sometime and shoot a game of pool together. It was just the kind of relationship they'd agreed upon. But all of a sudden, she felt oddly conflicted about it.

It was obvious that Cherie had struck a nerve in him. Perhaps the older woman had, too.

"Don't worry," she said, "you don't look the least bit married—at least by your definition. But I would advise you to stay away from Nicky and me. That tends to make women jump to conclusions."

He smiled wryly, then backed out of the parking space. He handled the Jeep with ease, as if it were a toy operating under his command. He was paying an inordinate amount of attention to his driving, it seemed to Hadley, as silence fell between them.

Neither spoke again until they were back on Aspen Street and in her driveway. He set the emergency brake firmly.

"Thank you once again," she said. "And once more, I'm sorry for disrupting your plans."

"No need to apologize. I was glad I was able to help," he said, getting out. Hadley stepped from the car and managed to open the back door before he could. Not wanting to delay Drake any longer, she began to unbuckle Nicky from his carrier.

"I'll lift him," he said, gently nudging her aside.

Grudgingly, she stepped back as he picked the boy up and held him to his side with one arm. "Good-bye, old buddy. I'm leaving you in charge."

Nicky, looking at Drake with rapt interest, smiled.

"Good-bye, Drake," Hadley said. "Enjoy what's left of your vacation."

He set the boy down. As Hadley took Nicky's hand, her fingers accidentally brushed Drake's. It was just for a moment, but long enough to turn her blood to fizz. She was close enough to pick up the scent of his freshly shampooed hair and feel the warmth of his body.

Drake grabbed the child seat from the Jeep and set it on the porch. As he began to leave, Nicky stretched his arms toward him and let out a howl.

"Dake!"

Drake, for all his training and tactical skills, stood frozen into place. He looked at Hadley helplessly.

She tightened her hold on the boy's hand. "It's all right. He'll be back," she said reassuringly. The wailing grew louder.

She glanced at Drake. His expression was unreadable. He stepped back, touched the boy on the sleeve, and without saying anything else, he strode away.

Hadley stood in the driveway, and stroked her son's hair. His crying dissolved to hiccups. She watched until the Jeep disappeared. Then came the sobering realization that her son had set his heart on something he could never have.

Approaching the outskirts of town, Drake kicked the Jeep up to fifty, and then braked with a groan. In his haste to salvage what was left of his vacation, he'd forgotten to check the gas gauge. It was sitting on empty.

A new convenience store appeared in the nick of time at the foot of a hill. He wheeled in and stuck a nozzle in his tank. The numbers on the pump started to spin, sort of like the thoughts in his head. Dirty diapers, burned soup, an appendectomy. Had this all really happened? A woman, a baby, an unwelcome confrontation with the past. Had he been the victim of some sort of cosmic joke?

The pump cut off, bringing him back to the present. A teenager wheeled up in a sky blue compact car, blue like . . . Nope, he didn't want to go there again.

Drake hastily hung up the nozzle and went inside to pay.

That done, he decided to grab some coffee for the road. At the other end of the counter a woman was making a cappuccino for the boy with the blue car. When she turned, a light flickered in Drake's brain. Her reddish-brown hair was now streaked with gray and she was thinner than he remembered, but he was certain that the woman was Callie Murphy's mother.

When he stepped up to the bar, the look in her eyes told him that she recognized him, too. "Mrs. Wycliff?"

"I don't go by that name anymore," she said tonelessly. "I've gone back to Murphy."

"Mrs. Murphy, I'm sure you remember me."

"Yes. Officer Matthieson. It's been a while."

"Yes, it has. How have you been?" He almost felt foolish asking.

"I'm getting by."

He glanced over his shoulder to make sure no one was within earshot. "I still check occasionally to see if there have been any developments in Callie's case."

"Thank you for remembering."

She'd been a vibrant, attractive woman when Callie disappeared. Now there were circles under her eyes and she looked pale and tired. Her hair, which had been as voluminous as her daughter's, hung limply about her shoulders.

Drake took a deep breath. "I'm sorry we weren't able to find her."

"I know you did everything you could."

An awkward pause followed. "I'll take a coffee to go, if you wouldn't mind," he said finally. "Black."

"Sure."

In the early days of Callie's disappearance, she'd worn a large button with her daughter's picture on it. Above it was the inscription, "Have you seen her?" When she turned back to hand him the coffee, her lapel was bare. Had she given up? There was so much he wanted to ask.

"That will be eighty-five cents, please," she said mechanically.

Drake handed her a dollar along with his business card. "Please let me know if you hear anything, or if I can help in any way."

"Thank you." With a forced smile, she slipped the card in her apron pocket and handed him his change.

He was almost out the door when she called him back. "I'm due for a break in a few minutes," she said. "Would you mind waiting?"

"Not at all."

He was standing aside, sipping his coffee, when Mrs. Murphy came up to him shortly afterward. She led him to a room in the back of the store and closed the door behind them.

"I know it has been a long time, but please don't let the police give up on finding my daughter." There was a pleading look in her eyes.

"The case is still active and there's no reason to give up," he reassured her. But he also knew that statistically, the longer a person was missing, the less apt they were to be found.

"She's out there somewhere. She's too smart to let anything bad happen to her. If only she knew that her stepfather was gone, I believe she would come home."

"Have you ever gotten any indication that Callie might be trying to communicate with you?" Drake asked. "For example, parents of some runaways have reported getting telephone calls in which the caller hangs up without saying anything."

"No, nothing like that." She took a deep breath as if she were trying to draw on some auxiliary source of strength. "But I just have this feeling in my heart. It's what keeps me going. Five years is such a long time to worry and wait."

Drake touched her shoulder. "I'm very, very sorry."

"You needn't be sorry for anything you did or didn't do. I don't hold anything against you or any of the other officers. I just wanted you to know that."

He gave her shoulder a squeeze. "That means a lot to me."

She glanced at her watch. "I'd better get back to work."

"Good-bye, Mrs. Murphy."

He strode out the door. If only he could let himself off the hook that easily.

CHAPTER FIVE

Aunt Margaret stood on the front porch looking tanned and fit—hardly the casualty of a tour bus breakdown. Wearing leggings and an oversized red sweatshirt with "Born to Boogie" on the front, she hugged her niece.

"It's so good to have you back, Aunt Margaret."

The older woman stepped inside. "It's wonderful to be back. While we were broken down in New Mexico, coyotes were howling in the hills. One of the ladies saw a desert rat and almost fainted. But once we were on our way, the bus company put us up free for the night and treated us to a very nice breakfast. Actually, it was rather exciting. On top of that, I met two attractive gentlemen. They both asked for my phone number. Tell me what's new with you. And let me see that darling grandnephew of mine."

She plucked Nicky up off of the rug where he had been playing with building blocks. As she covered him with smacking kisses, he turned red-faced fussy and squirmed out of her arms.

Hadley made green tea, Aunt Margaret's favorite. It had reputed health benefits and her goal was to live to be one hundred. She poured it into cups from her thrift store mix of Blue Willow and Currier and Ives china and they sat at the dining room table.

"While you were gone, I had a bit of an adventure myself," Hadley said. "I had an emergency appendectomy."

Aunt Margaret gasped. "Oh, my goodness, child. If I'd

known, I would have come back right away."

"It would have been hard, Aunt Margaret. You were out in the middle of who knows where. By the time you got here, the situation would have been mostly under control."

Hadley told the rest of the story. "So, you see," she concluded, "everything worked out anyway. The policeman was literally a lifesaver. Because of Drake, I had all the help I needed."

The older woman set down her teacup. "Drake? You don't mean Drake Matthieson, do you?"

Hadley's cup stopped between her saucer and her lips. "Yes, why, do you know him?"

"He started out as a rookie in Mountain Spring. He stopped me for speeding over on Cedar Avenue. He made me late for my hair appointment."

"I'm surprised you remember his name."

"Honey, every other woman in town probably remembers his name," she said, brushing a tendril of tinted red hair from her eyes. "He created quite a stir. A good-looking bachelor like him always does when he comes to a small town.

"I was old enough to be his mother, of course, but I could still see what the fuss was about. A few of the girls even tried to get themselves arrested. They'd speed, take out a taillight bulb or some such thing, just to get his attention. But he didn't seem to have much of an attention span. He'd date one girl a half dozen times, then he'd go off to another."

She paused for a moment, as if she'd had a particularly harrowing thought. "He's not still single, is he?"

"Yes."

"Well, it's a good thing his rescue mission is over," she said. "Let's hope he won't be back."

Hadley looked at her uneasily. "I'm afraid he will be. Three weeks from Saturday, as a matter of fact."

Aunt Margaret's eyes narrowed. "What do you mean?"

to be a kid whose world had been turned upside down.

Ben had already had a few scrapes with authority. He'd knocked out the front tooth of a boy who had been teasing him about his physique, and he'd been with a group caught spray-painting school busses.

When Drake had first met the boy, he'd been withdrawn and distant. But over time, the kid started to come around. Drake knew he'd turned a corner when the kid confided to him he liked Callie. And, well, he'd heard that Drake knew something about women.

It made sense that the boy would be attracted to Callie. She didn't fit in, either, but Drake suspected it was by choice rather than circumstance. Drake suggested that Ben break the ice by stopping by the school art studio after classes and complimenting her on her work. Maybe he could study up a little on art and ask her what she thought of whomever.

After a few visits, the kid worked up the nerve to ask her to a movie, but she turned him down. She claimed she had a boyfriend out of town. Sensing, as an insecure adolescent would, that she had invented the boyfriend to spare his feelings, he took the rejection hard.

Two days later, Callie disappeared.

It was Callie's stepfather, Stuart Wycliff, who forced a connection between the two events. Here was a kid from a troubled background who had been spurned. The seeds of suspicion he'd sown rattled an already-shocked community and left Drake sickened. There was no evidence to suggest Ben had anything to do with Callie's disappearance. Instead, Drake suspected Wycliff was trying to deflect any blame from himself.

Ben's pain was Drake's own. The boy took a lie-detector test and passed, hands down. But the damage to an already-fragile ego had already been done. Ben was never quite the same after that. After graduation, he quietly joined the Army. Eventually,

Drake had lost touch with him.

This all reminded him why he tended to avoid long vacations. They gave him too much time to think.

Hadley sat in front of her computer screen, designing a logo for a new gourmet pizza restaurant. Pizza made her think of Drake, and the trampled bits of it she'd picked out of the living room rug after he'd left. Unfortunately, a lot of things made her think of him. He'd been gone for five days. Why she was keeping count, she wasn't sure, but she knew that a man like that didn't leave without making a lasting impression. If only the dreaded hoedown were over and she could worry about more important things like that funny noise in the engine of the minivan.

She turned her attention back to the logo, changing the background from green to red, then back to green again. Just as she got back into the proper artistic frame of mind, the oven timer went off, followed by the doorbell.

She jumped up, pulled the sheet of sugar cookies out of the oven, and slid them onto a cooling rack. Then she rushed to the front door. She'd been expecting an overnight packet from a client. What she got was Drake.

She could see him through the quaint little multi-paned window in the front door. His dark hair was rumpled, as were his clothes, and he appeared not to have shaved since he left. She wondered how anyone who looked so bad could look so good.

"Hi," he said after she reluctantly opened the door.

She noticed immediately that he smelled like fish.

"How are you feeling?" he asked.

"Still a little sore, thanks, but I'm pretty much back to normal."

"Good. I've got something for you." He reached down and held up a dented bucket with holes in the top. "Trout. Two

beauties. However, not the record-breakers I was hoping for."
He lifted the hinged lid just enough that she could see a silver
tail flash.

"They're alive," she gasped.

"That's the freshest kind. You clean them and eat them right
away or you put them in the freezer."

She put a hand over her mouth and looked worriedly at the
bucket. "Can't we just take them to a petting zoo or something?"

Playfully, he rolled his eyes. "If you'll let me in, I'll do the
dirty work."

Before she could respond, he was into the living room and
headed toward the kitchen. She ran after him in order to keep
up with his long strides. "You're not going to do it in my kitchen
are you? Because if you are, I'm going to leave."

He set the bucket in the sink. When he turned back toward
her, his eyes glistened mischievously. "Shall I call you when I'm
finished?"

She stared at him a moment before nodding. "I'll be in
Nicky's room. He's taking his nap."

Losing no time getting there, she opened the door quietly in
order not to disturb him. She found him lying on his stomach
in his nearly outgrown crib. His dark lashes were fanned against
one exposed cheek. His rosy mouth was slightly ajar. Hadley sat
in the rocking chair next to the crib, watched his shoulders rise
and fall, and watched the wonder that was her son.

It had taken her a good five minutes to quiet him the day
that Drake left for the Killarney. His tears had caught her off
guard, making her realize how easily children could form attachments.

Yet he was only two, much too young to understand what
was missing from his life. So the tears could have been merely
those of a child in need of a playmate. Hadley wanted very
much to believe that.

She heard the door click open and turned.

"It's safe to come out now," Drake said softly.

She rose from the rocker. He glanced over her shoulder at the sleeping boy, paused for a moment, and then without saying anything, followed her out of the room.

"I cleaned up, too," he said. "You'd never know it was a murder scene."

"Make light of it all you like," Hadley said.

"Thank you, I will." He stood by the sink. It sparkled. The bucket was gone.

He was finished and soon to be on his way, taking those broad shoulders and that sexy stubble with him, Hadley thought with some relief.

"Now that you're the proud owner of some very nice pieces of fish, may I have a cookie as a reward?"

Her hopes for his imminent departure popped like a bubble. His gaze went from Hadley to the cookies, then back to her again. A faint smile touched his lips. Little smiles seemed to be the best he could do, given the tough world in which he navigated. The grudging quality of them added to their appeal. This time, she caught the slightest glimpse of strong, straight teeth, which looked exceptionally white in contrast to his shadowed face.

She couldn't say no. "Would you like some milk to go with them?"

"How did you know?"

"Boys are much the same, regardless of their age."

He peeled off his fishing vest, rolled it up and set it outside the kitchen door. It was then that Hadley noticed the bucket sitting out there as well. It was an unneeded reminder that he was a man for whom unpleasant tasks were routine. He was a man willing to take chances, to get his hands dirty. Hadley took no risks, not even talking on the phone during a thunderstorm.

She put the warm cookies on a plate and set two glasses of milk on the small kitchen table. It was a sturdy thrift store find which she'd decorated with folk art to cover some of its nicks, burns and gouges. Next to Drake's large frame, it suddenly looked delicate.

"Your trip to the Killarney was obviously a success," she said.

He nodded absently, appearing more interested in the sugar cookie that he had half demolished in one bite. "Delicious." A pause followed. "My mother made cookies like these. I haven't tasted any like them since."

Hadley thought of how profound his loss had been and her heart seemed to sink within her chest. "They're Nicky's favorite," she said.

"Mine, too." He picked up another one.

Hadley, not entirely delighted to hear that, got up and put a second sheet of cookies into the oven.

"You know," he said, inspecting the treat, "I would have had you pegged as whipping up something more exotic—maybe cookies with nuts found only in the Rain Forest three days out of the year."

Hadley folded her arms over her chest. On one hand, was a scorched black and white checkered mitt. "Just how else do you have me pegged?"

"I'd say that cooking up things with strange ingredients is as close as you get to having a wild side." He said it in the smooth, off-handed way of a man who had probably analyzed more women than Freud.

She gave him a look of warning. "That's who I am and I don't intend to change."

Suddenly, a whimper came from the direction of Nicky's room. Drake laid down his third or fourth cookie. Hadley had lost track.

"Why don't you let me get him?" he said.

Before she could protest, he was up and gone. She didn't want Nicky startled by the presence of a relative stranger. But her fears were unjustified. Not only was there a sudden absence of crying, but when Drake entered the kitchen carrying him, Nicky's eyes were positively alight.

"Here's your boy, just in from the land of nod."

Hadley reached out to take him, but he pulled back against Drake. She felt a twinge of dismay. He not only remembered Drake, but some sort of male bonding had already taken place. Over the boy's protests, Hadley reached once again for her little traitor and plucked him out of Drake's arms.

She kissed him on the cheek. "Let's have a cookie and some milk." She settled him down in his high chair next to the kitchen table. She could feel Drake's eyes on them.

"Looks like I've got myself a buddy," he said.

She turned to face him. "Drake, I don't want him to get too attached."

His gaze, as gray as an overcast sky, locked on hers in mutual understanding. "I'll be careful." He quickly finished another cookie and got up. "We're still on for the hoedown, aren't we?"

"I'm afraid so."

He gave her a chiding look. "Believe it or not, I'm not a bad date."

"It's not a date, remember? It's a deal."

"I remember. By the way, they dress Western. Jeans will do fine."

He touched the cowlick on Nicky's crown, gave Hadley a quick wave and was gone.

Suddenly, the kitchen seemed very quiet and very empty. Even Nicky, who looked at her quizzically, appeared to notice. A restless anxiety began building in her veins. To dispel it, she began putting things back in order even though she wasn't finished baking the cookies. For a man who didn't want a family of his own, he fit in with her family much too well.

Aunt Margaret showed up a few weeks later with a flat box marked "Property of Mountain Spring Community Theater."

"I want you to try this on," she said.

Hadley, who had been in the middle of designing a restaurant menu, looked at her warily.

The older woman set the box on the dining room table and took off the lid. She parted a few layers of tissue paper and lifted out a dress by the shoulders, letting the hem fall to the floor.

It was a green, orange and purple plaid with a high, ruffled neckline and leg-of-mutton sleeves. The bodice had chunky green buttons down the front and came to a point at the waist. At the hem was a deep ruffle with touches of white eyelet underneath. It was awful.

"You want me to put that on?" she asked.

"Honey, it's from *Oklahoma!* I got it from my friend, Wilma. She's in charge of costumes for the community theater. It would be perfect for the hoedown. A lot of the girls wear long dresses."

Hadley, trying to hide her distaste, touched the fabric. It had a scratchy, synthetic feel to it. "It's very sweet of you, Aunt Margaret, but I thought I'd just wear jeans. That's what Drake suggested."

"He would. They'd show off that nice little behind of yours."

Hadley's mind was still muddled from the tedious list of Italian names on the menu. But it was clear enough for her to be mortified. "I'm not sure I'm following you."

Aunt Margaret touched a well-manicured hand to her throat. "Don't you see? No matter what you call this arrangement you've got with Drake Matthieson, it's still a date. And if you're going out with him, you can't afford to look too appealing. He probably has enough ideas of his own without giving him any."

She held the dress up against Hadley's shoulders. "These are not your colors."

"They're nobody's colors."

"And the tight bodice will emphasize the fact that you're not terribly well-endowed."

"Aunt Mar-gar-et," she groaned.

"That means the dress is perfect. Go ahead," she urged. "Try it on."

Hadley stared at it for a moment before taking it. Hesitantly, she unzipped the back and slipped it on over her yoga pants and t-shirt. Aunt Margaret got behind her and gave the zipper a quick run upward. The dress fit perfectly, except for being a bit tight around the neck and a fraction of an inch too short.

"Let me look at you," she said, standing back. She twisted her rose-tinted lips in scrutiny. "You look wonderful—from the neck up."

Hadley planted her hands on her hips. "All right, Aunt Margaret, you've had your fun." She reached to undo the zipper.

"I was just trying to help," she said, giving her a quick, but warm hug. "I didn't mean any harm."

She responded with a slow smile. "I know you didn't."

Hadley wriggled out of the dress, folded it and put it back in the box. She handed it to her.

"Just keep it," she said, handing it back. "Wilma's retiring it."

"No, thanks," she replied, setting the box down.

Ignoring her, Aunt Margaret grabbed her rhinestone-spangled tote bag from a chair and started toward the door. "I'll be here to baby-sit around seven-thirty. I'm looking forward to it." And then she left with an energetic flourish.

Hadley stared at the box, uncertain what to do with it. All she wanted was for Saturday to be over.

Jeans suited Hadley better. With them, she wore a white cotton shirt, a red bandanna and hiking boots—the closest she had to the cowboy variety. It was decidedly an understated look, entirely no-nonsense. The mirror confirmed that. She wore no make-up except mascara. Instead of lipstick, she'd opted for clear gloss. There would be no giving this man ideas.

Aunt Margaret was sequestered in Nicky's room when the doorbell chimed. To calm herself, Hadley had been drawing from her Lamaze training by taking deep breaths and exhaling slowly. But that didn't stop the sound of the bell from sending her heart scampering up to her throat.

She took another breath and opened the door.

He stood on the porch wearing faded jeans that hugged his lean, powerful body with subtle sensuality. His shirt was also white, but of the pearl-buttoned Western variety. Tied loosely at his throat was a navy blue bandanna. A Stetson was cocked provocatively over one brow. Missing was the cop's decorum. In its place was a hint of roguishness and devil-may care. He was so dangerously appealing that the wall of reserve inside her threatened to crack.

He studied her with slow and deliberate interest before taking off his hat. "Look at us—a matched team."

Her cheeks warmed. She thought of couples that sometimes dressed alike to make a statement of love and unity to the world. "Actually, I'm not quite ready yet," she finally managed to say. "I still have to change."

He looked mildly puzzled. "What do you mean? You look terrific."

He stepped inside. He smelled faintly of soap and freshly cut cedar, the same scent that he'd left on her pillow.

"Please sit down," she said, trying to ignore his deep gray gaze. "I'll just be a minute."

In her bedroom, she peeled off her jeans and tossed her shirt on the bed. She grabbed the box Aunt Margaret had left and quickly wriggled into the garish plaid eyesore that passed for a dress. The fabric was so loaded with polyester, that wrinkles hadn't stood a chance. For a split second, she perversely entertained the notion of keeping the hiking boots on. But her better instincts prevailed and she substituted a pair of black ballet-style flats. She gave herself a cursory glance in the mirror. This would surely zap the gleam out of his eyes.

It didn't, at least not perceptibly. When Hadley entered the living room, her skirt rustling, Drake drank in the view. "Very nice," he said, rising.

Hadley looked at him cautiously. "You really think so?"

"Of course. Green and purple are my favorite colors."

She stifled a sigh of exasperation. "Thank you—I guess." Was it possible for a man who headed a SWAT team to be color-blind?

Perhaps it was just his deftness at complimenting women. It was second nature to him, since he'd had so much practice. He was so good at it that he only had to sacrifice part of the truth. Surely, that was it. He couldn't possibly like the dress.

He helped her into his Jeep, billowing skirt and all. He tossed the Stetson into the back and pulled away from the curb. "Do you know how long it has been since I've been out with a woman?"

Hadley felt a kick of alarm. "This is not a date. It's a deal, remember?"

He cast her a sidelong glance. "Sorry. What I was trying to say was that it has been a year or so since I dropped out of the game. It had something to do with turning thirty-five and a lot to do with the fact that most of the eligible women were at least ten years younger. About your age, as a matter of fact."

Hadley relaxed slightly. "Sorry if this is like having to take your little sister to a dance."

He shrugged a solid shoulder. "You're young, Hadley, but

you're older than your years. Probably because of things that have happened."

She bit the inside of her cheek, unable to disagree. "Do you feel older because of . . . ?" There was no need to finish the sentence.

"Yes, I do. Always have."

She stole a glance at him in the darkness. The light coming into the car from the street softly rimmed a nearly perfect profile. His jaw was square and stoically set. His eyes were trained on the road ahead. His hair, somewhat ruffled, gave him a boyish look that belied his stern expression. She felt her heart go over a bump in her chest. Like it or not, their common experience had forged a bond between them. He drove past the lights and turn-of-the century storefronts of Mountain Spring and headed toward Denver. About ten minutes out, he exited onto a country road that cut through miles of pasture. In the distance, Hadley could see a barn with light streaming through the hayloft and the front doors. Cars surrounded the building. Hadley began to hear strains of fiddle music.

Drake drove through the main gate of the ranch and followed a gravel road to the back of the barn with a sureness that suggested familiarity.

"You've been here before, haven't you?"

"Lots of times."

"With a different woman every time."

He paused as if to contemplate her question. "Yes, I'd say so. But last year, I didn't go."

"What did you do instead?"

"I stayed home and watched baseball on television. That's what I usually do on weekends now, other than fishing, reading suspense novels and working out in the police gym."

She looked at him, surprised. "You're really serious about taking yourself out of circulation?"

"Absolutely."

Hadley wasn't sure she believed him. His tone had been firm, but there was a hint of mirth in his eyes. Only one thing was clear: When it came to women, Drake Matthieson was unavailable for the long term.

He parked the Jeep next to a hay wagon. Hadley opened the door to prevent him from doing it for her. But the distance she'd put between them closed alarmingly when she suddenly felt his hand at the small of her back. An unwanted sensation of warmth went scurrying up her spine. He bent down and whispered in her ear as they strolled into the weathered building. "My cautious one, it doesn't get much safer than a barn full of cops."

Inside, Hadley didn't feel safe at all. Although they weren't in uniform, she instinctively knew who the officers were. If it wasn't in the breadth of their shoulders, or their agile movements, it was in their bearing. Even in the merriment of the moment, with music playing and feet shuffling, she could sense a bit of reserve, a remnant of decorum. Despite their strength, skill and prowess, they were as vulnerable as Quint had been. Feelings she'd worked so hard to bury began working their way to the surface.

Drake slipped his arm around her shoulder just as the live band finished its slow country tune. "Let's take care of business first. There's the commander. Let me introduce you."

He led her to a tall, well-built man with iron-gray hair and craggy features. Although his expression was stern, his pale blue eyes radiated kindness. His arm encircled the waist of a middle-aged woman with short auburn hair and a pale green square-dance dress.

"Matthieson," the commander greeted with a friendly swat to the arm. "Good to see you, Lieutenant."

Drake smoothly went through the formalities of introduction, after which they engaged briefly in the benign chatter of the newly introduced. Afterwards Drake and Hadley moved on to a table laden with refreshments.

"Thanks," she said.

"For what?"

"I'm glad you didn't say anything about my being part of the police family, so to speak."

"This wasn't the time."

She offered him a grateful smile. A slow country tune began to wend through the air.

He set down his empty cup. "Let's dance so the commander will have something to report back to Mitzi."

Before she could respond, he swept her into his arms in one easy, practiced motion. Her heartbeat quickened as he drew her against his firmly muscled body, leaving just enough of a niche for her to place her head next to his. Guardedly, she held back, but she was still close enough to feel the heat of his skin next to hers.

But she couldn't pull her hand away. It fit into his as if it belonged there. Her pulse was so strong that she was afraid he could feel it.

He led her gently across the dance floor and in the headiness of the moment, she'd forgotten about wearing what was easily the ugliest dress there. For a moment, she'd almost forgotten she was dancing with a cop, a womanizing one at that. She pulled away slightly.

"What's wrong? Did I step on your toe?" His eyes, normally a cool, clear gray, were warm.

"No, I was just thinking."

"A thinking woman. I've always liked that type."

"You like all types," she reminded him.

He smiled wryly. It was a tight, but arresting smile, one that could make a woman stop whatever she was doing. Even her.

But she kept going, maintaining as much of a distance as she could for being in a man's arms. When the music stopped, she pulled back, only to have him embrace her once more when the band started up again.

From around the square shield of his shoulder, she studied the nearby dancers. A young, blond woman had both arms around her partner's neck. An older couple, their movements not so fluid, smiled at each other. She overheard a young wife mention their child's latest antic as she looked into her husband's eyes.

Suddenly, the past began to rush in on her as she contemplated the merriment around her. Would the couples grow old together or would their time together be cut tragically short? As she pondered the question that lurked deep in the heart of every policeman's wife, her hand tightened involuntarily on Drake's shoulder.

"Could we go outside for a bit?" she asked when the music stopped.

He held her at arm's length. His eyes were murky. "Are you feeling OK?"

She nodded. "It's just that . . . I just need to catch my breath a little."

With his hand at her elbow, they made their way toward double doors flung open wide into the night. Near the exit, three young women stopped talking as they approached. One looked at Drake with blatant interest. The others looked at him, then at each other in tacit approval. To his credit, Drake seemed not to notice.

Yet she knew these were the types of women that he belonged with once he got back into circulation. And she was sure that he would. They were fresh, fun loving and spontaneous. They were unencumbered by mortgages, children, or minivans that made suspicious noises.

Outside, the air was springtime crisp and smelled faintly of blossoms. The moon, almost full, washed the surrounding pasture with light.

"I have an idea," Drake said. "Let's take a drive and look at the rest of the ranch. We might even run into some of the buffalo."

"What about the dance?"

"Are you sure you want to return to a barn full of cops?"

Hadley hesitated.

He touched her elbow. "You were very quiet. I could guess what was probably going through your mind."

"I'm all right," she insisted.

"You've returned the favor. I'm off the hook. I won't ask any more of you. I'll even take you home, if you like."

Suddenly, Hadley realized how much she needed this diversion. As much as she loved her son, she often yearned for an extended conversation with an adult. Drake had been kind to her and had given generously of his time. She owed him more than just a brief appearance at a dance.

"A drive through the ranch would be nice," she said.

The Jeep took the bumpy gravel road with ease as they drove past acres of grassland. On the horizon, the faintest trace of mountains could be seen.

"After the accident, I used to come out here and ride. The owner kept a stable of horses for city kids. At the time, I was living with an uncle in Denver. We weren't getting along, with my being a moody teenager and his being quick-tempered. So, I'd spend every Saturday I could on horseback. I rode an old gelding named Charlie and we were a team—real pals. I told him my troubles and he always listened."

A light laugh escaped from his lips, but in it, Hadley sensed a tinge of bittersweetness. Her heartstrings tightened.

Drake stopped the Jeep. "Let's get out. I'll show you something."

She slid out the passenger's side, dragging after her yards of tangled plaid, and joined him on the narrow, rocky road. He slipped an arm around her shoulder and stopped, turning her slightly.

"See the tallest peak over there?" He pointed to the night-shrouded mountain range.

Hadley nodded, but her attention was focused more on the heat of his fingers radiating through her sleeve.

"What do you see?" he goaded. "Use your imagination."

She pretended to study it, but Drake's nearness was playing havoc with her concentration. "It looks like meringue on a pie, with the tall peak in the middle," she said finally.

"I used to call it 'Peak Porpoise.' It looks like a porpoise rising up through the water. The surrounding peaks are the waves. I used to make a game of it—sort of like cloud reading. Your mind can roam free out here."

Suddenly, he dropped his hand from her shoulder and walked a few steps ahead. He stopped at a fence, pulled off a length of a wild vine and knotted the ends together. When he turned back toward her, there was something irresistibly boyish in his grin. She realized that in him, at that moment, was the boy that he'd missed out on being.

He stood in front of her and placed the wreath around her neck. In his eyes, she saw a glint of mischief. She mustered a look of wry impatience.

Ignoring it, he leaned over and kissed her.

CHAPTER SIX

At first, the kiss was tentative, the slightest touch of his lips on hers. It was as if he were giving her an opportunity to say no. But Hadley was too stunned to say anything. The gentle heat of his mouth on hers sent her blood on a stampede through her veins, leaving her dizzy and senseless.

He pulled her closer and deepened the kiss, his fingers playing through the ends of her hair. She answered his need with her own by touching the rough, angular plane of his jaw. His pulse jumped under her fingertips. For an instant, she forgot why they shouldn't be in each other's arms and yielded to his embrace. It was a man's embrace, long missing from her life.

Her mind grappled as her senses struggled against reason. Then came the sharp chill of reality. She twisted away, pushing her hands against the solid expanse of his chest. "Please, don't," she said, her heart hammering in her throat.

He gave her a long, searching look, his gaze intense. "I'm sorry."

Hadley pulled the wreath from around her neck and regarded him warily. "That makes two of us."

An uneasy silence hung between them, one that spoke louder than words. He was the first to break it.

"I'd be lying if I said I didn't enjoy it."

Hadley's heart gave a little kick. Rather than admit the same, she said nothing.

"I'm sorry, Hadley," he repeated.

"I accept your apology."

He smiled stiffly. "I hope we can still be friends."

She nodded, although she was uncertain that even that was wise.

They talked on the way home but said little. They talked the innocuous talk of strangers—a little about the weather, a lot about the merits of small-town living. Throughout the charade, Hadley's heart still strummed, her lips still tingled.

Drake pulled into Hadley's driveway just behind Aunt Margaret's little red convertible. Just as he switched off the engine, a single louver opened on one of Hadley's shuttered living room windows. After what seemed like a very long minute, it snapped shut.

"A wary woman, your Aunt Margaret. I heard she was a ball of fire in the neighborhood watch program."

Grudgingly, Hadley smiled for the first time since Drake had kissed her. "Be careful. She's got you in her sights now."

He turned toward her. "I know she probably wonders what I'm up to, but it's your opinion I'm most concerned about—especially after tonight."

"There's nothing to worry about. There hasn't been a woman in your life for a while. There hasn't been a man in mine . . . It was just one of those things."

"Right. One of those things." He walked her to the front porch and turned toward her. "Thanks, Hadley. Thanks for helping me maintain a decent relationship with my commander. Thanks for not complaining about my dancing. Thanks for overlooking my foibles—at least for one night."

"That's nothing compared to what you did for Nicky and me."

He shrugged. "Helping people is what my job is all about." A beat of silence followed. "Bye, Hadley. Maybe we'll see each other around sometime."

She nodded. "Maybe we will."

He reached out and touched the awful leg-of-mutton sleeve on her dress, its colors even more garish under the yellow porch light. Then he turned and left. When he did, the night seemed to go very still.

Inside, Aunt Margaret was sitting on the sofa reading a magazine, although not very convincingly. It was a graphic arts trade publication, filled with technical information about software upgrades and color separations. Aunt Margaret didn't know a pixel from a Popsicle. She hated technology.

"Oh, hello, dear," she greeted, slapping the magazine shut. "How was the hoedown?"

"It seemed like a good time was had by all. How's Nicky?"

"He didn't want to go to bed, so I put on a CD of Sousa marches and we pretended to be in a parade. It took about twenty laps around the living room, but I finally wore him down. He's been asleep for about an hour."

Hadley sat down next to her. "What would I do without you?" she asked with a laugh.

Aunt Margaret reached over and gave Hadley's hand a quick squeeze.

"Do you plan to see Drake again?"

"No."

Her eyes widened. "I do hope he behaved himself."

"Of course he did," she said, tweaking the truth. "Aunt Margaret, it wasn't a date, remember? I owed him a favor."

"Debt paid, account closed, right?"

"Right."

Aunt Margaret seemed to relax a little. "Did I tell you there's a new dentist in town? He's Stella Waldrop's grandson. He graduated fifth in his class at the University of Colorado School of Dentistry. He's got a tiny camera that can show close-ups of your teeth on a TV screen."

"And he's single," Hadley added.

Her eyes brightened. "How did you know?"

"I didn't, Aunt Margaret. I just know you."

She sighed. "Hadley, I don't mean to meddle, but Drake is the first man you've gone out with since you lost Quint. I just thought maybe you'd reached a turning point."

She shook her head. "Drake isn't a turning point. He's a dead end."

Aunt Margaret laughed. "Oh, my wise girl. For him you've got to be a first."

"How's that?"

"This has to be the first time he's encountered a woman who can resist him."

If she only knew, Hadley thought ruefully. For a few seconds, she too, had been unable to resist. Just how could that have happened?

The next evening, as she pushed Nicky in his stroller past the neat little bungalows on Aspen Street, she was still pondering that question.

She had come up with several explanations: It was a fragrant spring night and her hormones had gone awry. It had been too long since she'd felt a man's arms around her. It was only chemistry and nothing more. But that didn't change the fact that emotionally, she'd wandered right smack into a danger zone.

She'd come to Mountain Spring to raise her son in relative safety, away from the harsh Dallas streets where his father had died. She'd become a woman who looked both ways twice before going through a green light, who examined toys for sharp edges and loose parts, who tossed out anything even a couple of days before its expiration date. She'd become a woman who took no chances. And now, just as she'd tamped her feelings down to a comfortable numbness, Drake had come along. The cocoon she'd spun around herself had cracked, leaving her vulnerability exposed.

It was not until Nicky emitted a squeal of delight that she realized that the stroller was fairly flying, powered by the dynamo of nervous energy that churned within her. She slowed and turned the stroller around, to find that Mrs. McBee in the little yellow house across the street was watching her with interest. She stood in her flowerbed, with her trowel in one hand and a clump of weeds in another. Feeling slightly foolish, Hadley waved and kept going, this time much slower.

Drake's parting words replayed in her head: "Maybe I'll see you around sometime." Hadley shook her head as she wheeled down the sidewalk, leaving a puzzled Mrs. McBee behind. Friendship pact or not, maybe even "sometime" wasn't a good idea. The kiss had changed everything. But if that was what it took to sever the connection between them, perhaps it was a blessing in disguise. If a man were to awaken feelings in her, let it be someone who shared her need for a safe, orderly life. Drake's life was the antithesis of that. His was a bold and reckless taunting of danger.

She couldn't face another loss or even live in dread of it. When Quint had died, she'd stopped believing in tomorrow. In the raw, nightmarish days afterwards it was hard to do the simplest tasks, like getting out of bed in the morning. She struggled to put one foot ahead of the other. She'd almost stopped eating.

Then there was the bittersweet news of the pregnancy. Only then was she able to move out of the haze of her grief. The joy of birth overshadowed the tragedy of loss. The first time she looked in her son's eyes, everything changed.

She was afraid of friendship with a man who took on police

work's most dangerous assignments. She was afraid of Drake. Too much exposure to his dark good looks and grudging grin could be dangerous, even to a hardened and wary heart like hers.

And worse, he was a delight to a little boy who would soon understand the absence of a father. She didn't want Nicky to lose twice.

The raid was planned for four the following morning. That was bedtime for most meth lab operators who plied their felonious trade while their neighbors were asleep. That was the best time to catch them with their guard down, discounting the inevitable pack of attack dogs.

Drake, dressed in dark pants and a matching regulation t-shirt, sat at a table in the squad room. He strummed a surveillance photograph of the crack house with the eraser end of a pencil. He'd just held a strategy meeting with his SWAT team. The last man had just left. He was alone, with only his thoughts to keep him company.

The thoughts he was having weren't very good company. He was thinking about kissing Hadley. He needed to be thinking about his work instead.

Before, he'd always been able to compartmentalize. He could focus on the job to the exclusion of all else. After hours, he could devote unwavering attention to the blonde, brunette or redhead of the evening. If not that, the sports page or a good steak.

The problem with Hadley was that she hit too close to home, home being that place in his heart that he kept sheathed in iron. Seeing her in her little beehive of domesticity was one thing. Squiring her around the dance floor was another.

Her body was compact, slender and surprisingly warm considering the cool side to her personality that she hadn't hesitated to show him a couple of times. The little dip at the base of her spine was the perfect fit for his hand. Up close, unlike some women, she still looked good. What you saw was what you got. The best he could detect, there was no makeup to camouflage any flaws. Given that and the high-necked schoolmarm dress, he wondered if she was trying to tell him something. He hoped that wasn't a message to men in general. He'd hate to see all that girl-next-door wholesomeness go to waste. And that reminded him. There were nine years between them. Although she was very much a woman now, she had been in middle school when he'd entered the police academy.

Drake pushed away from the table, got up and began pacing over the tiled floor in his military-style boots. He wasn't sure what had come over him that night. He wanted to dismiss it as lust, but deep down, he knew it was more than that. She was starting to mean something to him.

He nervously massaged a spot over his heart as he tracked back and forth. She'd answered his need with her own. That made two of them who were sorry. He'd heard it said that the fear of something—in his case, commitment—could be like a magnet. It seemed to put out negative ions, attracting the very thing you were trying to avoid. No stranger to discipline, he wasn't going to allow that to happen to him.

Hadley owed him nothing now, if she ever did in the first place. Whatever had passed between them could now be nipped safely in the bud. That was it. He wouldn't see her again. And that would be doing both of them a favor.

He sat down to complete some unfinished paperwork. He barely got started before the phone rang. It was the commander.

"Lieutenant, could you come in my office?"

An uneasy feeling spread over him. "Yes, sir."

Commander Benson seldom called individual officers into his office unless it was serious. He usually met officers on their own turf, whether it was in the squad room or the gym.

Drake found him at his desk. On the shelf behind him, among other family photos, was an eight-by-ten glamour shot of his daughter, Mitzi. She was outfitted in a froth of red feathers. He pretended not to notice.

"Sit down," he said, pointing to a chair in front of his desk. He was about ten years older than Drake, but the responsibility of running an entire division had etched deep lines in his forehead, making him look slightly older. They'd been close when they were partners—Benson a family man and Drake the department playboy. He'd been part father, part older brother. Benson knew almost as much about him as he knew about himself. In the days they rode together, he gently urged him to settle down.

"You're a good man," he'd said more than once. "As a cop, you're true blue. Find the right woman. It will make all the difference in your life." The memory of this blitzed through his head as Drake sat down. Nervously, he crossed one long leg over the other.

Benson leaned forward. "The young lady that you were with at the hoedown . . ."

Here it comes, Drake thought, fighting the urge to wince. *Don't let him be inquiring on Mitzi's behalf.*

"Yes, sir."

"Did I correctly understand her to say that she was a graphic artist?"

"Yes."

"That's what I'm looking for. At least, that's what my wife says I need. Wanda dabbles a little in art herself, but she's the oil painting type. Likes old barns and country scenes."

Drake's stomach tightened as he wondered where all this was leading.

"Anyway, she says graphic design is a different ball of wax.

They do stuff like that on computers now. What the department is looking for is someone to redesign our squad cars. You know, new logo, stripes, detailing, that sort of thing. Something that looks sharp. Headquarters has a new fleet of cars on order and Wanda suggested a makeover. She says our old cars are boring. The name of the department looks like it was spray-painted on with a hardware-store stencil. I spoke to the chief about it and he likes the idea. All we need now is an artist. The sergeant said that this young lady's husband was a cop. He remembers her from the appendix incident. Being of the fold might give her an edge. Would you talk to her about it?"

Drake felt like he'd just swallowed a cannon ball. He opened his mouth to speak, but he didn't know quite what to say.

"You're not seeing her anymore?" the commander asked.

Drake's gaze shifted to the general vicinity of Mitzi's brass-framed picture.

"Well, it's not anything really official. We're friends, though."

"Good, then you can be in charge of the project." Benson picked up a file folder and shoved it toward him. "This might give her some ideas. Inside are pictures of squad car logo designs from Santa Monica to Tulsa. I'd like to get this going as soon as possible. The new fleet is scheduled for delivery in six months. In the meantime, we need to get together a logo committee."

Drake picked up the folder as if it were a bomb set to detonate in the next five minutes. Going back to Hadley's and seeing mother and son with those matching cornflower blue eyes was the last thing he wanted to do.

"Yes, sir."

Being a good cop, that's all he could say.

Hadley looked at the washing machine and felt the sudden onset of a headache. Water seemed to be leaking from its every seam. At her feet, yards from the nook where the washer and dryer sat, a small lake formed on the kitchen floor. Suds oozed up from under the lid and slid down the front of the washer. This would have to happen on a weekend when repairmen charged double time, that is, if they would come at all.

Nicky, wearing his last pair of clean overalls, let out a yelp and made a dash for a mound of suds drifting their way. Hadley barely caught him by hooking a finger in an overall strap. But when she did, his feet went out from under him, pulling her down with him. Her bottom hit the tile with such a thump, that the roots of her hair seemed to vibrate. Water soaked her khakis through to her skin. She wanted to cry, but Nicky beat her to it.

At first it was a whimper, then it escalated to a full-blown, roof-raising howl. Her gut in a knot, Hadley scrambled to her feet and gathered Nicky in her arms. She'd just managed to get him settled on her hip when the doorbell rang.

"Perfect timing," she grumbled as she hobbled, dripping, through the dining room, then the living room. Nicky's wet overalls were quickly soaking what little of her khakis remained dry. After several attempts to turn the doorknob with her one free, but wet hand, she flung open the door. She looked up and her heart kicked. It was Drake. Nicky's howling stopped instantly.

Their eyes met in one flashing moment, then Drake's gaze moved slowly down her body. She shivered as a cool, spring breeze washed over her.

"Seems I've caught you at a bad time," he said dryly.

"No, everything is fine, under control." She brushed back a tendril of damp hair that had stuck to her cheek. She certainly didn't need him to hang around and help.

His eyes, full of mischief, sparkled. It was obvious that he didn't believe her.

Suddenly, he reached out and took Nicky from her arms. The little defector went straight to him with a gap-toothed smile.

"Would it be too nosy for me to ask why the two of you look like you've been attacked by a monster water balloon?"

"The washing machine sort of blew up."

Without waiting to be asked in, Drake was over the threshold in one powerful stride. He set the toddler down gently and made hasty tracks toward the kitchen. Nicky started to whimper. Hadley took the boy's hand and followed.

In the kitchen doorway, she froze in mid-step. The entire floor now lay under a sheet of water. One of Nicky's toys, a plastic baseball, bobbed in a corner.

Her nerves dancing, Hadley went briskly to the utility closet and took out a mop and bucket. When she returned, Drake was pulling wet laundry out of the washer, wringing it out and setting it on top of the dryer.

He looked at the hoses in the back. "I'd guess the pump has gone out," he said. He reached into the tub again and pulled out a padded and underwired lace bra of modest dimensions.

Hadley set the mop and bucket down with a splash. "I'll handle that." She treaded across the room and snatched it out of his hand. The motion was punctuated with the pop of elastic.

He raised an eyebrow and a slow smile spread across his face. "Don't worry. There's nothing that you wear that I haven't seen before."

"Countless times, I'm sure," she snipped. She checked the tub to see if anything was left.

"Countless? As in the stars in the sky and drops in the ocean?"

Hadley shot him a look of impatience, gathered up the wet laundry in a basket and set it in the bathtub. When she got back, Drake was mopping up the water on the kitchen floor. She felt a pang of guilt.

"I'm sorry." She touched her temple where a headache was getting worse.

He looked up and rested his hands on the mop handle.

"There we go again. It seems like we're always apologizing to each other. We're supposed to be friends."

"It seems as though we still haven't gotten the hang of it," she said. Only Hadley knew she couldn't. The solution to the problem of Drake Matthieson was to keep him away, but he kept coming back into her life like a heat-seeking boomerang.

"We might have to get the hang of it," he said.

A rivet of concern went through her. "What do you mean?"

"I'll explain later. Right now, let's get this mess cleaned up."

With a sense of foreboding, Hadley went into the bathroom, got a stack of towels and began tossing them on the kitchen floor to help absorb the water. She didn't know how much longer she could be "friends" with him. His lips tasted of spice; his arms encircled her as if they were made for her body.

When it came to Nicky, she gave love boundlessly, and no matter how much she gave, she had more to give. But when it came to loving a man, that reservoir of her heart was empty. She'd loved Quint and he was gone. She thought no one could take his place—until now.

Drake had opened up the possibility that she could actually grow to love someone else. And that frightened her, because in loving, there was a good chance of feeling pain once again, pain that cut to her very soul.

She swabbed furiously, glancing up only occasionally to check on Nicky. During her dark musings, he'd somehow gotten hold of a feather duster and was using it as a mop. Mimicking Drake, he pushed it back and forth, pausing occasionally to shake its dripping fronds over the mop bucket. Most of the water went back on the floor.

"That's the way, buddy," Drake said. "You're a good partner."

Nicky beamed up at him, and then went back to work. Drake continued on, handling the mop with surprisingly smooth efficiency.

"How did you come to be the master of the mop?" Hadley inquired.

He stopped in mid-sweep. "In a foster home. My foster parents got as much housework out of me as they could—before school and after. On the upside, I lived in what was probably the closest you could get to a germ-free existence."

Hadley felt her heart sway. "You didn't tell me you were in a foster home."

His expression was guarded. "There's not much to say."

"I thought you had relatives."

"I did—and do. It's just that while they were squabbling over who was going to have to take me in, I had to stay somewhere. I was only with the foster family about three weeks." He mopped absently over an area which had already been mopped. "After that, I stayed with one uncle, then went on to stay with two more. At least, I never got tired of the wallpaper at any particular place."

His attempts at humor seemed to mask what could only have been a traumatic experience. For a moment, Hadley was at a loss for words. "It must have been hard."

He shrugged. "It taught me to make the best of whatever hand I was dealt."

She gazed at him. His shoulders were square and strong, his back straight. She imagined him as a young, untethered tree that had stood up to the wind and come out stronger for it. Suddenly, she was filled with admiration.

He paused, leaning on the mop handle. "Come to think of it, you've never told me anything about your family."

"Nicky is about it, except for Aunt Margaret. My parents died some time ago. I was an only child. My mother was forty-six when I was born. To say that I was a surprise would be the world's biggest understatement."

"I can imagine. And Quint's parents?"

"His father is in the military, stationed in Japan. His mother died before Quint and I were married. He has a sister in Alaska."

Uncomfortable talking about anything that might make anyone feel sorry for her, she quickly changed the subject. "Thanks for helping. You didn't have to."

"No problem. Glad to do it." He stepped out the back door to empty the bucket of water. Nicky followed with his feather duster.

Hadley surveyed the floor. It was still wet, but there was no standing water. Only a trace of suds remained around the washing machine.

Drake returned with Nicky tagging behind. "Now that we've finished swabbing the deck, I'll tell you why I came."

He leaned against the machine, bracing himself with both hands behind him, and casually crossed one ankle over the other. Nicky clumsily leaned against the dryer.

"My commander wants to know if you'd be interested in doing a design project for the police department."

She felt a mix of anxiety and surprise. "What sort of project?"

"They want to redesign the markings on our squad cars."

"Drake, did you have something to do with this?"

"No. Honest."

"Then, why me?"

"The sergeant who was on duty during your medical emergency told him of your police connection. The commander thinks that's important."

She bit the inside of her cheek. The project would thrust her back into a world that had brought her so much sorrow. She glanced at the washing machine. The repairs could be expensive, assuming it could be repaired at all. How could she turn down an opportunity to earn more money? How could she turn down a high-profile project, one that could result in business-generating publicity?

"I'll see what I can do," she said.

"Good," he said.

Instead of appearing satisfied, however, he looked mildly troubled. He strode into the living room and picked up a folder he'd left on a table near the door. He came back and handed it to her. "Here's something for you to look over."

She opened it to find photographs and a cover letter from the district commander. "I'll be working with the commander?" she asked hopefully.

Drake nodded. "But I'm the liaison. Mostly, you'll be working with me."

CHAPTER SEVEN

Drake came back the next afternoon, this time in a black and white squad car.

Through the open shutters in the bedroom she'd converted into an office, she watched him get out, closing the door with an authoritative snap. As he strode up the brick walk lined with yellow jonquils, his mouth was set in a straight line. This was not a social call.

Before he could reach the porch, he was intercepted by Mr. Knickerbocker from next door.

Hadley took Nicky by the hand and stepped outside. It seemed that Drake was having to account to Mr. Knickerbocker for his presence.

"Are you and that little feller all right?" the old man asked, his gaze shifting to her. His white hair formed an iridescent halo around his head.

"We're fine, Mr. Knickerbocker. I'm just going to do some artwork for the Police Department. I appreciate your concern."

"Sorry to give you a scare," Drake said.

"That's quite all right." He gave Drake a polite nod and walked stiffly away.

"He's very protective," Hadley explained, once he was out of earshot.

Drake responded with one of the brief, grudging smiles that she was beginning to like all too much, then his expression turned businesslike again. "Well, let's get to work."

Hadley, mildly relieved by Drake's quick attention to the matter at hand, took photographs and measurements of the squad car. All the while, having Drake's six feet-plus of lean sensuality so near made it difficult to concentrate.

Just as she jotted down the last of the dimensions, a large drop of rain from the leaden sky fell on her notepad. A few more splashed down in quick succession, followed by a hard, pelting torrent interspersed with pea-sized hail.

Drake grabbed Nicky and the three of them made a dash for the front porch. Hadley, with her denim shirt soaked nearly through at the shoulders, looked out into the yard in amazement. The squad car was a black and white blur, its outline barely visible through the downpour.

She turned to Drake, his well-toned body all too clear. His hair glistened. His cheekbones had taken on a dash of color. In his arms was Nicky, looking all too snug and content.

"At least the storm had the consideration to wait until you finished your calculating," he said. "What do you think? Will it be possible to spiff up the old black and whites, to make uncool look cool?"

"Of course," she said. But she wasn't thinking about patrol cars and logos. She was thinking about him and how utterly sexy he looked holding her son.

"Do you think you could come up with something in the next six to eight weeks?"

"I might be able to do a little better than that." If she had to work nights, she would in order to finish the project as quickly as possible. The sooner she did it, the sooner she would be done with Drake.

"Good. I'll tell the commander that we've got things rolling." Nicky's head was now lying against his shoulder.

"I'll do several designs," she said. "The committee can select what it likes best."

"Sounds like a plan."

For a moment, they stood in silence, watching the beaded curtain of rain that wrapped around the porch. The drops danced on the sidewalk, giving a silver sheen to everything they touched. The jonquils drooped under their weight.

Her gaze shifted to Nicky. And it was then she noticed a tear on the shoulder of Drake's t-shirt. Below, on his upper arm, was a deep scratch. It looked fresh. She had a sudden impulse to touch it.

"How was your day?" she asked instead.

"Interesting. For one thing, I pulled over four little old ladies. I caught them ripping through a hospital crosswalk doing at least fifty. Pedestrians scattered out of the way. One on crutches barely made it. The next thing I saw was the blur of silver fins from an old Cadillac."

Reminded that police work could have its lighter moments, Hadley smiled despite herself. "Why were they in such a hurry?"

"They were late to a charity luncheon. When I refused to excuse them on that basis, one in the back seat got sassy. She waved her purse at me and threatened to report me to the mayor, the police chief and my mother. She said I was interfering with charity work."

"What did you do?"

"Nothing, at least not to her. I figured it was just the sherry talking. Judging from her breath, she was well into her second or third cocktail hour. I had to summon a patrol officer to ticket the driver. I was concerned that the people at the next crosswalk might not be so lucky."

"The terror with the purse didn't give you that scratch, did she?"

He glanced down at his arm. "No."

She looked at him expectantly.

"We made some arrests early this morning," he said after a

pause. "One of the subjects had swallowed some of the evidence. That's how I came to be at the hospital. Exactly how I got the scratch, I'm not sure. All I can say is that he didn't take kindly to being apprehended."

She looked at the minor wound again and a little ache coursed through her. "Are you sure you're OK?"

He smiled crookedly. "I'm sure." He set Nicky down. "If there's not anything else you need on the car design, I'll go. You have work to do and I need to get some rest. If you have any questions, give the commander a call."

"What about fees? We haven't even discussed that."

"Discuss it with the commander. His number is in the file."

She looked at him quizzically. Suddenly, the realization hit. He didn't want to be here any more than she wanted him here. Drake touched Nicky's yellow hair. "So long, old buddy."

He gave Hadley a quick wave and turned. But before he could step off the porch, a popping sound came from the side of the house, followed by a metallic crash.

Hadley's stomach lurched. She dashed to the end of the porch and looked around the corner. A long section of rusted gutter dangled from the edge of the roof. Water poured off the shingles, down the side of the house and onto a window.

"Oh, no," she groaned.

"Oh, no," Nicky mimicked.

She glanced over her shoulder at Drake. "My grandmother had a saying that trouble comes in threes. The washing machine was one. This makes two."

"I'll call Wayne," Drake said.

"Who's Wayne?"

"The dispatcher for the Mountain Spring Police Department. He moonlights as a handyman. He can have you fixed up in a day or so."

"Drake, really. I can call. You've got more important things to do."

He looked at her, and then at Nicky, then his chin crinkled as if he were having a bothersome thought. "I'll see that he gets in touch with you."

Saying nothing else, he made a dash for the squad car. Hadley watched as he pulled slowly away. Thank goodness he didn't volunteer to fix the gutter. She'd been wrong about it being trouble number two. It was trouble number three. Trouble number one was Drake.

Drake sat on his sagging brown sofa with a carton of carryout chicken on his lap. The television was on, but only for the sound of another human voice. Hockey wasn't his game.

He had to do something. Hadley was dangerously close to wiggling her way into his heart like no woman ever had before. And she wasn't even trying. That's what really got him.

Despite having been up since three o'clock that morning, sleep was the furthest thing from his mind. If he went to bed, he might think of how cold and empty his bed was. There were women who would be glad to provide the warmth he needed, but he found himself wanting Hadley.

There was something about her that reached beyond just primal need. He tossed the drumstick he was nibbling back in the box and set the box on the coffee table. The table in his cubbyhole of a dining area was piled with magazines and newspapers he'd never bothered to clear off. Besides, it was lonely eating at a table for one.

On Hadley's table, there was a starched, white tablecloth with some sort of lacy loops set at an angle across gleaming wood. The place smelled of furniture polish and lemons, but what he noticed most was the way she smelled. Even at her worst—up to her ankles in soapy water—she had a calming floral scent that made him think of spring flowers. At least that's what he remembered from the few times he'd stopped to smell them.

And food tasted better there. Even a sandwich. Even scorched soup.

A warning siren howled in the recesses of his consciousness. A rescue mission was in order—a mission to rescue himself.

Drake got up and fished the "G" file out of a desk drawer. At random, he opened the alphabetized red book with worn edges. Melanie Henderson. Moved to Texas. He turned another clump of pages. Debbie Logan. The name had a bold "X" over it. Debbie had a cousin in the diamond business who could get great deals on rings—engagement rings implied. Stay away from that one.

He turned the page. Jodi Mason. There was a real possibility. She was past thirty and philosophically opposed to marriage. Why didn't he think of her before?

He snapped the book shut. He'd fix up his apartment; maybe learn to cook a little. He'd hop back in the saddle again.

Hadley waited for the better part of the day for a call from Wayne the handyman, but it never came. One to two more inches of rain were predicted for that night. She understood the difficulty a dispatcher would have in making a personal call. She would just have to be patient.

But it was the doorbell, and not the telephone, that rang. Halfway expecting to find a stranger, she found Drake instead. Her heart tumbled over on itself.

He wore jeans slightly torn at one knee. His faded plaid flannel shirt was rolled up to the elbows, revealing thick forearms. His eyes were shadowed, as if he hadn't slept well. If anything, he looked a little grouchy. He held a toolbox.

"Drake," she said in surprise.

"Give me a half hour and I'll have your new gutter installed. A few nails, a few clips, and I'll be done."

Hadley looked over his shoulder to see a section of gutter protruding from the back hatch of his Jeep. "Drake, you shouldn't have. I thought . . ."

"Wayne broke his leg in a motorcycle accident yesterday. He won't be climbing ladders for a while. Speaking of ladders, you have one, don't you?"

"In the garage."

She'd barely said the word before he was gone. For a moment, she stared, baffled, at the empty porch. He hadn't been in that big of a hurry to get to the Killarney.

Restlessly, she went to the kitchen to check the stew she'd put in a cast iron pot earlier in the day. After giving it a stir, she went back to her office with Nicky so she wouldn't be distracted by the sight of Drake's long legs through the living room window. It was enough to know that he was there, prying and hammering, as if his presence needed any more announcing. Her pulse was reacting like a silly teenager's, bumping crazily in her chest like a pinball.

She tried to keep a pleasant face for Nicky's sake as she taped printouts of several versions of a company logo on the wall. She stood back to assess them from a distance. But in her mind's eye, she saw only Drake.

What could she tell him, not to come back again? That she was feeling things that he obviously wasn't? She took a long, deep breath and held it a minute before letting it out. She had too much pride for that. He was just doing what good cops do—helping the family of a fallen comrade. She was just experiencing a pure and not so simple case of yearning. Too many nights alone could do that to a woman.

She plucked the center logo off the wall and went back to the computer for a minor revision. Before she could finish, she heard the back door open.

She went to the kitchen to find Drake with a handkerchief tied around his left hand.

"Could you spare a Band-Aid?" he asked.

Instinctively, she reached for his hand. When she saw the spot of blood on the handkerchief, her hand went to her mouth. "What happened?"

He pulled off the wrapping. "Just a little metal cut."

She took his hand delicately in hers for a closer examination. The cut, between his thumb and forefinger, was not so small and slightly jagged. "I'm so sorry. Come to the bathroom. I'll get you fixed up."

Nicky appeared in the doorway, towing a small yellow locomotive on a string.

"Hey, buddy," Drake greeted.

Nicky smiled and offered him the toy.

Drake re-wrapped his hand and examined the little train with exaggerated interest. "That's an impressive piece of machinery you've got there," he said, returning it.

Nicky reached for the handkerchief.

"Drake has a boo-boo," Hadley explained. "Mommy's going to make it better."

The three of them in the bathroom made for close quarters. Hadley got out hydrogen peroxide and a box of plastic bandages. Automatically, she took Drake's wrist and held his hand over the sink before she realized what she was doing. She was so accustomed to attending to Nicky that she'd instinctively tried to mother Drake as well. When she felt his heartbeat under her fingertips, the heat of her own pulse rushed to her cheeks. Without looking at him, she poured the peroxide unsteadily over his hand.

Nicky, on tiptoes, peered over the sink. "Mommy, kiss boo-boo."

Hadley uprighted the bottle so abruptly that the antiseptic splashed into the sink. Her gaze shot to Drake. A smile sneaked across his lips.

"Kiss boo-boo," the toddler insisted.

"What do you say? Can't a guy get some first-class medical treatment around here?" Drake angled a cheek as if daring her.

She shot him a look of annoyance.

He eyed her playfully. His gaze was almost as pale as smoke and Hadley struggled not to get lost in it.

Quickly, she blotted his hand with a cotton ball and plucked a bandage out of the box. She jerked off the protective wrapping, revealing a bright green bandage with purple dinosaurs on it. She slapped it over the cut.

"Ouch," Drake said. "Is that the way to treat a wounded man?"

"There you are, Lieutenant," she said, ignoring his question. "In a few days, you'll be almost as good as new."

"Thank you, Nurse Happy Face. Come on. I'll show you your new gutter. I'm almost finished."

She took Nicky's hand and followed Drake. He stopped in the middle of the kitchen. "Something sure smells good," he said, eyeing the pot on the stove. "What is it?"

"Stew—from a Greek cookbook."

He looked at the pot wistfully and then lifted a towel draped over the countertop. Under it, rose two rounds of homemade bread. "Sorry, force of habit. Cops tend to be nosy, you know."

Hadley also remembered that they tended to be hungry, especially at the end of the day. She felt a pang of guilt that reached all the way to her sneakers.

There he was, bandaged, hungry, and probably tired, not only from doing his own job, but from doing one of hers. He couldn't help it that he stirred unwanted feelings in her. It wasn't his fault that he was an all-too-attractive symbol of her past and present fears.

"Stay for supper, Drake." She couldn't believe she was saying it.

"I couldn't. Mrs. Martinez might turn a missing person's report if I didn't show up for the tamale special at La Cocina. I'm one of her regulars."

Hadley felt a wave of relief that was quickly overshadowed by a subtle twist of disappointment. She absently lifted the cloth covering the bread. "Maybe some other time."

She looked up to find him eyeing the dough. Then his gaze cut to hers. "On second thought . . . Thank you. I'd like to stay."

They stepped outside where a section of shiny new gutter hung over the dining room windows. With his hands on his hips, Drake looked at it proudly.

"That looks wonderful," she said.

"I wish I could say that for your rose bush."

Hadley glanced behind the ladder to see part of it snapped off at the base. Her shoulders sagged.

"Sorry. I'll get you another one," he said. "I stepped on it."

"Don't worry about it," she said, pretending it didn't matter. It was a special-order antique variety. She'd just bought a trellis for it, but hadn't had time to put it up.

She went back to the kitchen to finish supper as he finished up outside. There they were, working together as though he belonged here. But both of them knew he didn't.

He came in just as she was taking the bread from the oven. His hair was ruffled from the wind. Across one cheekbone was a dark smudge. In some haphazard, all-male way, he was more appealing than ever. Without taking her eyes from him, Hadley set the bread down, accidentally setting it on top of the toaster.

"If homemade bread is my reward, I'll replace all your gutters. I'll rake your leaves, wash your windows and rotate your tires."

"Save yourself the trouble," she said, trying to ignore his arresting smile. "Buy some frozen dough."

He stepped up to the counter to get a closer look and casually slung an arm over her shoulder. Her pulse jumped.

"But it wouldn't be the same," he countered. "Dough from the freezer case could have been made by a man with dirty fingernails and falling cigar ashes."

"I doubt it. There are standards, you know."

"You should be the standard. You could start your own brand and put your picture on the package. That's all it would take to hook a few million starving bachelors."

Hadley gently removed his hand from her shoulder. Even touching it lightly, she could feel the strength in it. "Drake, you're wasting your charms on me."

His eyes dimmed slightly. "Sorry. Old habits die hard."

A look of understanding passed between them, making words unnecessary. "It's OK," she said reassuringly.

He nodded and turned away. She could see his firm thigh muscles at work underneath his jeans as he walked toward the dining room. Across the rug, Nicky pulled a small, squeaking red wagon with a lone passenger—his teddy bear.

Drake crouched on one knee and complimented him on his driving.

Hadley sensed in Drake an obligation to be a positive influence in the life of a fatherless boy in the way that the highway patrolman had been in his. Drake was wonderful with Nicky. And if that weren't enough, he was taking a small can of oil from his toolbox and tending to the squeaky wheel. He turned the wagon upside down, administered a few drops, and then spun the wheel until the squeak disappeared. Nicky looked up at him, his eyes round with total and innocent fascination.

What a simple thing Drake had done, yet how complicated were its implications.

At supper, Nicky sat at the table with them. Repeatedly, he offered Drake pieces of carrot out of his stew.

"I know what you're up to, little guy." He picked up the boy's spoon and popped the carrots into his mouth. Nicky ate them without protest.

"Ironic, isn't it?" Hadley said.

Drake tucked the spoon back in the boy's fist, and looked at her quizzically. "What's that?"

"You've got a way with kids."

He shrugged. "You know, I've never had better stew," he said, quickly changing the subject. "Or bread."

"Thank you." She'd already guessed his approval. He'd eaten heartily—two large bowls of stew and a half round of bread, slathered generously with butter. He'd also emptied two glasses of milk.

They'd said little of consequence during the meal. Nicky was a much-needed diversion from Drake's dizzying sensuality. But now, he was yawning widely and rubbing his eyes with his plump little fists.

The boy didn't take gladly to the suggestion of bedtime. His face screwed up with the imminent threat of tears. Hadley lifted him out of his chair, but he reached out to Drake. "Get in bed like a good boy and I'll sing you a song," he said. Hadley turned to Drake in surprise.

"Well, it worked last time," he said with nonchalance.

She readied Nicky for bed, outfitting him in pajamas that looked like a baseball uniform. Drake turned down the bright patchwork quilt on his crib and propped his teddy bear next to his pillow. They worked together as if they were a team—like partners, like parents, Hadley thought with dismay. She didn't need anything else to make her heart turn to Jell-O over a

117

daredevil cop with a playboy past.

He leaned over the rail of Nicky's crib and started to sing:

> *Hey, little cowboy*
> *Hang up your hat*
> *Kick off your boots*
> *It's time for a nap . . .*

His voice was deep, rich and melodious, containing a surprising hint of emotion. It wrapped around her like warm silk. Rats. Did he have to be able to sing, too?

> *There's adventure awaiting*
> *On the wide prairie*
> *So rest up little cowboy*
> *There's so much to see.*

> *There are maidens to rescue*
> *And wild horses to tame*
> *. . . Spin a few ropes*
> *And practice your aim . . .*

He stumbled over a few of the lyrics, giving the song a bumpy cadence. Hadley couldn't help but smile.

> *Rest easy little cowboy*
> *Everything will be fine*
> *Ride off in the sunset,*
> *Leave your troubles behind.*

When it appeared that Nicky was asleep, Drake bent down, and with a moment of hesitation, kissed him on the crown.

Suddenly, a lump rose in her throat. She turned away and rushed toward the door, but it was too late.

"Hadley," he said softly, following her.

Just as he caught her by the arm, she turned out the light so he couldn't see the tears that had sprung to her eyes. She pulled away and strode into the living room, quickly wiping her eyes with the back of her hand.

He took her by the shoulders and turned her to face him. "You were thinking about Quint, weren't you?" His eyes were dark with concern.

"I'm sorry," she said, purposely not answering his question. "I don't know what came over me." And she didn't. All she knew was that the tenderness that Drake showed Nicky had shot straight to her heart. At that moment, the truth became inescapable. Something within her had changed. She realized that there was room in her heart for someone else. She could no longer hide behind grief, or loyalty to a memory.

What she should have been experiencing was a feeling of freedom and hope. But it was so very frightening when it was the wrong man who was kissing her son.

CHAPTER EIGHT

Drake kept a bottle of aspirin in his desk for days like this. He took two, chasing them down with a gulp of black coffee. In his division alone, a branch bank had been robbed, several senior citizens had been scammed, and a sports car had been stolen, leading officers on a not-so-merry chase through the suburbs of Denver. They got their man, but not before the culprit plowed into a squad car, totaling it. He usually thrived on such chaos, losing himself in the excitement of it. But he found himself thinking about Hadley at the worst moments. Just this morning when that stolen sports car was hurtling down the expressway at the speed of light, he worried that a certain green minivan might be in its path.

He thought of the dimple in her cheek and the way the kid's eyes lit up at the sight of him. He thought of her home-cooked meals. And each time, it sent a bolt of fear through him as if he'd suddenly found himself looking down the barrel of a fugitive's gun.

Damn, he hated that he made her cry. He had only meant to soothe Nicky. The song had worked before. Instead, he'd gotten the mom crying. It had taken him a few moments to understand why. It was Quint who should have been standing at that crib, not him.

He took a deep breath. He remembered his vow to get back into circulation again. Just maybe he'd take Detective Grayson up on his offer to check out that new singles bar.

The telephone offered a timely and welcome diversion to his thoughts. He snapped up the receiver before it completed its first ring.

"Drake . . ." Despite the noise in the background, the voice sounded vaguely familiar. "It's Ben—Ben Talbot."

Drake leaned forward in surprise. "Ben! It's been ages. Where in the world are you?"

"I'm at Ft. Hood, Texas, but tomorrow I'll be headed your way. I'm on leave and I'm going to visit some friends in California. I've got a stopover in Denver tomorrow night. If you could get away and meet me at the airport, it would be great to see you."

"I'll be there." Drake scribbled down the flight number, hung up, then leaned back in his chair. It had been years since he'd heard from the kid. The fact that he still meant something to him left him a little bit short of amazed. Then he remembered that Hadley had said he was good with kids. Mentally, he kicked himself for allowing her to creep into his thoughts again. He needed to quit procrastinating and get back to living like the carefree single that he used to be.

Ben was waiting for him in full dress uniform. There were sergeant's bars on his sleeve.

"Hey, buddy," Drake said, giving him a cuff on the shoulder.

With a crooked grin, Ben gave him a swat in return. "Great to see you, Drake."

He stood back and assessed his grown-up "little brother" with a twist of pride. "It's good to see you, too. It looks like you've done pretty well for yourself."

"The military has been good for me."

As they stood in front of an expanse of plate glass, watching planes come and go, Ben gave him a brief update on his life. It included a completed tour of duty in a war zone. The voice that was once soft and stammering was now confident and clear. His scrawny adolescent frame had become full and muscular. Also gone was the adolescent complexion. His face was now smooth, tanned, and not a long shot from handsome.

"What about you, Drake? How's police work?"

"It hasn't lost its allure."

"Still have that string of babes?"

"I've slowed down some."

"You're not thinking about settling down, are you?"

"Nope." He thought of Hadley and put more emphasis on "nope" than he had intended. "What about you? Got a girl-friend?"

"Not at the moment."

He paused. "Drake, did they ever find Callie Murphy?"

Drake shook his head.

A muscle twitched in Ben's jaw. In the gesture was a remnant of the angry and defensive boy he'd been.

"I'm sorry you had to go through that," Drake said.

"I guess I was pretty bitter for a while," Ben said. "But I wasn't the only one having a tough time. Even after I was cleared, the stepfather never apologized. I always wondered why."

"It looks like that will have to remain a mystery," Drake said. "He died sometime back."

Ben blinked. "I didn't know."

Drake told him about running into Mrs. Murphy.

"She doesn't hold anything against me, does she?"

"No. She seems to be putting a lot of the blame on herself."

"Did she say why?"

"For remarrying too soon after Callie's father's death. My gut feeling has always been that it's more complicated than that."

"Yeah, it always is."

The boarding call sounded for Ben's flight to San Francisco.

The soldier responded with a tight-lipped smile. "Well, I guess I'd better be on my way."

"It's really been great to see you again," Drake said, feeling an unaccustomed rush of warmth. "Keep in touch. Don't drop out of sight for so long. If there's ever anything I can do for you, I will."

"I wish you could, but I'd be asking you to do something that no one else has been able to do."

"What's that?"

"Find Callie."

Drake swallowed hard.

"It was just a crazy wish," Ben added quickly.

Drake touched his arm. "No, it's not." The boarding call sounded again.

"Stay safe," Ben said. "You mean a lot to me."

Drake hugged him. Ben stepped back, gave him a snappy salute and turned away. He was just a few steps toward the gate when Drake called to him.

"Ben, I'm really proud of you."

The younger man's eyes glistened. "Thanks."

With a tightening in his chest, Drake watched him disappear down the flight ramp. Sure, he was glad to see the kid, but what had come over him? Self-respecting cops didn't go around hugging other guys. Unless, maybe, they were their sons.

Drake took off down the concourse. He passed a middle-aged couple who were apparently seeing their grandchild for the first time, while the infant's parents stood by beaming. Further down, a small boy with a balloon and hair like Nicky's rushed toward a man who had just stepped through the arrival gate. The kid's sneakers didn't even seem to be touching the ground.

At airports, they had newsstands, coffee bars and gift shops. Why did they have to have all this family stuff, too? Drake broke into a jog and took off for the nearest exit.

Hadley sat at her kitchen table in her bathrobe, eating a cranberry muffin and nursing her second cup of cappuccino. *The Mountain Spring Clarion,* with its list of weekend events, was spread out before her.

She double-checked the time of the Mountain Spring High School Art Show. For Hadley, art was always a good tonic for whatever ailed. It soothed, inspired, and temporarily distracted her from problems like Drake Matthieson. Her work used to be an escape, until she ended up with, of all things, a police car design project.

This year, the art show was dedicated to a missing girl named Callie Murphy. This spring marked the fifth anniversary of her disappearance.

Hadley studied the girl's photo in the paper. Her most striking feature was a wild profusion of light, shoulder-length curls. In her eyes was a glint of defiance. "An extraordinary talent," her former teacher was quoted as saying, "one that comes along only about once in an art teacher's career."

It seemed that Callie had just vanished one day, leaving behind a half dozen exhibit pieces, plus several unfinished projects. Investigations by police and a private eye hired by the parents had turned up little in the way of clues. Just imagining the anguish of Callie's parents made her heart ache.

Mountain Spring High School was a work of art in itself. Built in the Art Deco style of the 1930s, it had colorful decorative tiles along its beige brick façade and tall, paned windows. Hadley had admired it every time she drove by.

Today, there was a sweeping, lime green banner strung over the entryway announcing the art show in bold black letters. Clusters of students milled about outside, some with bizarre clothing and hairstyles. One kid's hair was configured into a half circle of spikes that resembled the crown of the Statue of Liberty. Another wore jeans that had served as a canvas for various colors of spray paint. They were held up by a chain and padlock.

There was something she admired in their bold and expressive creativity. As a student, Hadley's style had been more conservative and traditional. Her guess was that Callie would have belonged to their school, the School of Bold and Anything Goes.

Some of the girls smiled at Nicky as she pushed his stroller up a ramp leading onto the green- and white-checkered tiles of the main corridor. On one easel in the entrance was a framed and expertly calligraphed dedication to Callie Murphy. On another was her picture.

Hadley picked up a brochure, which said Callie's works, with the exception of a small, special exhibit in the art studio, were interspersed with those of other students.

In the main exhibit, student artwork hung along the corridor walls as far as she could see. Hadley joined an admiring group of viewers looking at landscapes. It made her realize that she missed the museums and galleries of Dallas, but she wasn't ready to go back. She wasn't sure she ever would be.

The first of Callie's works was a well-executed and finely detailed rendition of multi-colored irises in bloom, their heads leaning slightly in the wind. In the corner were her initials in a serpentine swiggle. The work was dated a year prior to her disappearance.

Hadley saw an abundance of student talent, innovation and creativity, but Callie's art stood out. She'd painted a still life of a pair of very worn cowboy boots. She'd done a surrealistic watercolor of a woman who seemed to be lost in a forest. There was a pen and ink drawing of a once-grand but dilapidated house. She seemed to have mastered every medium she tried. But what became increasingly obvious was that the more recent her works were, the stranger and more symbolic they had become. Hadley stood mesmerized in front of a composition in which heavy slabs of black, gray and white paint were used to form the image of a colorless garden in bloom.

"What do you think?" The question came from a very familiar male voice.

She spun around to find Drake standing behind her. He looked lean and outdoorsy in jeans, hiking boots and a gray wool sweater. A few strands of dark hair fell over his forehead. Her heart skittered.

"Drake, what are you doing here?"

"Shocked to see that I have a little culture?"

"Maybe."

He grinned crookedly, then reached down and tousled Nicky's hair.

Even the greenest rookie could have guessed that she might be here. Just what was he up to? "You haven't answered my question."

He hooked an arm around her shoulder and pulled her aside, making her pulse jump. "Come on, and I'll tell you."

He led her down an empty hallway, away from the crowd. "It has to do with Callie Murphy," he said. "I was on the force here when she disappeared."

Hadley didn't know whether to feel foolish or relieved that his presence had nothing to do with her. That he might be wrestling with some of the same feelings she was having . . . Well, she could put that thought to rest.

"You never mentioned that," she said.

"The fact we couldn't find her isn't anything I'm proud of," he said, his gaze darkening.

"But you did your best, I'm sure."

"Yes, I did. We all did, but that wasn't enough. She vanished a couple of weeks before I was to report for duty in Denver. Even in that period of time, we should have been able to locate her, but none of our leads panned out."

"Did she run away, or do you think she was abducted?" Hadley asked.

"My gut feeling is that she ran away. Take an artistic temperament and teenage hormones, and then throw in the death of her father. Add to that a stepfather she didn't like. What you get is a pot of emotions that could boil over at any time." His tone was cool and objective. He recited the facts of the case with a familiar cop-like reserve. But Hadley knew that his presence here said something else.

"Has her case been reopened?"

"It was never closed."

"You're not here on a police mission, are you?" She knew a cop couldn't stand to be on the losing side of a game of cat and mouse. After a while, it got to be a matter of principle.

"I'm not here in any official capacity. The case is long outside my jurisdiction."

"Then why did you come?"

"I've been thinking a lot about this case lately." A glint of amusement appeared in his eyes. "You certainly ask a lot of questions. Ever think of hosting your own quiz show?"

She shot him a look of impatience. Why couldn't he take that sexy gray gaze and go someplace else?

"Any other questions?" he asked.

She looked at him thoughtfully. "How could somebody just vanish for five years?"

"It happens. People obtain falsified personal identification documents. They stay on the move. They're sheltered by friends or find their way into the foster care system in one state after another. Once the kids turn eighteen, and there is no reason to suspect foul play, these cases usually end up in a back file gathering dust."

She understood, although accepting it was another matter. A gun-waving felon who was an immediate threat to peace and safety would always get priority over a wild child on the run. But that did little to ease a family's pain.

"What do you think of Callie's art?" he asked.

"She seems to work some sort of magic on everything she touches."

"Would you care to see the rest of her paintings with me?" he asked.

Hadley hesitated.

"Come on," he insisted. "Help stamp out art illiteracy. Be my guide. Better still, think of it as a public service. Maybe you can help me understand an open case through an artist's work."

Drake's presence seemed to charge the air around her, setting off sparks of emotional conflict. But how could she say no? If anything, seeing the depth of the girl's talent had deepened her interest not only in the art, but in the renegade artist herself.

There were three more of Callie's paintings in the main exhibit. One was a parody of Van Gogh's "Bedroom at Arles." But the room contained one thing that Van Gogh's didn't: a television set. "You can't say she doesn't have a sense of humor," Hadley said.

"She didn't show it the day I gave her a ticket. She tore it up and threw it out the window."

"What did you do?"

"I stepped back so she wouldn't run over my foot."

He turned his attention to a black canvas with nothing on it but the signature of someone named Brittany, the *i* in her name dotted with a circle. He scratched his head and moved on.

The next oil painting was Callie's, a beautifully rendered scenic entitled "Autumn Glory." Strangely, however, it was done in black, white and gray. "She's gone color blind again," Drake said.

"It's attention-getting, isn't it?" Hadley asked.

"Artists should keep things simple—like you do."

Hadley looked at him in surprise. "You noticed my watercolors?"

"Sure, I couldn't help it. They were right there above the fireplace."

"Did you like them?"

"Yep."

She pressed him further. "Is there anything in particular that you liked about them?"

"Well, for one thing, a tree was a tree and a mountain was a mountain. And it was all in color."

"Thank you," she said, trying to suppress a grin. It wasn't the most sophisticated and knowledgeable critique she had ever gotten, but she was struck that he'd even ventured close enough to see her signature.

"Your pictures are . . ." He suddenly looked slightly flustered. "Well, I'd say . . . pretty."

Her insides turned soft. Just what she didn't need—another reason to be drawn to him. "That's very nice of you to say."

Drake looked uncomfortable and quickly changed the subject. "Let's go on to the special exhibit."

Hadley had to quicken her pace to keep up with him.

The special exhibit of Callie's unfinished works was in the school's art studio. Hadley studied the works carefully while a small crowd milled around. One was experimental and drastically different from what she'd seen before. The girl had been attempting to cover a globe with clippings from newspaper headlines. The headlines were all somber; with news of wars, crimes and death. About a third of the globe had yet to be filled in. A box of clipped headlines sat next to it on a worktable.

The last two were rough sketches. One showed a clothesline with a family's clothing twisting in the wind. The other showed a pair of very worn high-top baby shoes.

The baby shoe sketch stirred something in Hadley. It was more than a mother's sentimentality, but she couldn't pinpoint it.

"Flowers in black and white, a world covered with bad news . . . That would be pretty consistent with a runaway's frame of mind," Drake said as they strolled outside. Suddenly he stopped. Hadley looked up to find a middle-aged woman. She was dressed simply in a white blouse and black pants.

"Hello, Mrs. Murphy," Drake said.

"Hello, Lieutenant. I didn't expect to see you here."

"Callie has been on my mind lately." He briefly introduced Hadley, and then told Mrs. Murphy about seeing Ben.

"When I checked with the local police to see if they had any new information, they told me about the art show," he said.

"It was nice of you to come," she said.

"She's a wonderful artist," Hadley said, taking care to use the present tense.

Mrs. Murphy looked wistfully at Nicky. "Even when she wasn't much older than this little fellow, I could barely keep her in crayons. I don't know where she got it. She certainly didn't get it from me."

"Did she talk much about her art?" Hadley asked.

"No. I tried to talk to her about it. Maybe I didn't know how to ask the right questions. I didn't understand the more modern stuff. That's what she was doing before she . . . left."

Hadley wanted to reach out and give her a sympathetic embrace, a show of support, but she held back, sensing an uneasy reserve in the woman.

"Well, I'd better go inside," Mrs. Murphy said. "I wanted to thank her art teacher personally for remembering her."

Drake shook his head as Mrs. Murphy faded into the crowd. The morning sun glinted off his dark hair. "Heartbroken mothers. They're always tough to face."

"Drake, who's Ben?"

"It's a long story. Let's sit down." He led her to an empty concrete bench underneath a large oak tree. Hadley listened to Ben's story so intently that she realized she was staring. Was this consummate cop capable of deep feelings after all? Or, had he just been trying to keep a kid out of trouble?

As the story unfolded, it appeared that the boy actually meant something to him. She could see a glint of pride in his eyes as he described how snappy he'd looked in his uniform.

At the same time, the relationship was oddly arm's-length and sporadic. That's the way it would be for two men who had known such loss as boys. When in danger of getting too close to anyone, they would always retreat back to a safer distance.

"After seeing Ben, I guess I came here to take a very long shot in the dark," Drake said. "I thought there might be a remote chance that there could be someone here who might appear to know something about Callie, someone who might inadvertently draw attention to themselves."

"Like returning to the scene of the crime?"

"Something like that."

"Did you see anyone of interest?"

"You," he said playfully.

Hadley gave him a look of warning. "Drake . . ."

"No, no one with a cloak and dagger."

His expression turned serious. "There was a guy who bought one of her pieces the week that she disappeared. We checked him out thoroughly. It turned out he was a forty-ish interior decorator still living with his mother. By all accounts he had no interest in women, let alone a pistol like Callie. He was just a collector who had seen her stuff at a regional high school competition in Denver. He had a proven history of buying artwork there."

"Was her art teacher of much help?"

Drake shook his head. "Not really. That Callie would leave behind unfinished work before a major exhibit was incomprehensible to her. She said Callie didn't confide in her about her personal life. But she did note that she had been spending more and more time in the art studio after school. It got to where the janitor had to ask her to leave so he could lock up."

"It sounds like she didn't want to go home."

"All signs point to that. The mother and stepfather both acknowledged there were problems, that she resented anyone taking her father's place. But they insisted things had improved, that the situation was never bad enough to make the kid want to hit the road.

"The stepfather was pretty vocal about his dissatisfaction with the police. We checked computer and phone records. The Denver Police Department turned the art scene there upside down and shook it. We called out dogs and helicopters. We questioned everyone who could possibly know anything, including Ben.

"That's when Stuart Wycliff, her stepfather, got fixated on Ben. Unfortunately, there was that one piece of circumstantial evidence that gave his suspicions some legitimacy. Ben was a rejected suitor, so to speak.

"Ben's foster family vouched for his whereabouts during that time period, but that still didn't satisfy Wycliff. When Ben voluntarily took the lie detector test and passed, I thought that would be the end of it, but I was wrong. The stepfather suggested the results might be a false negative. Ben retook the test and the results came up the same. But it wasn't enough to erase the trauma the kid had been through."

"Did you ever doubt Ben?"

"You can't be a cop without being a skeptic," he said. "The circumstantial evidence concerned me, but there was something in his eyes and his voice that told me that he was telling the truth. I think he would have rather died himself than have harm come to that girl."

"Poor Ben," she said. "You think he still cares for her?"

"Yeah, I do. Kids like him don't form attachments easily. In fact, they try to avoid them. But once they do, they have trouble letting go."

Hadley noted a masked look in his eyes. He was talking about Ben, but she wondered if he could have been talking about himself as well.

"Did Callie actually have a boyfriend—like she told Ben?"

"She had a few male friends, but not an actual boyfriend as best we could tell. The art teacher had never heard her mention anyone, neither had her parents or her friends. Nothing turned up in her e-mail. She must have told Ben that to let him down easy."

"Did she take any clothes with her?"

"Apparently just what she wore. On the day she left, she was wearing ordinary clothes—jeans and a black turtleneck sweater. That was odd, because most of the time, she looked like a member of Sgt. Pepper's Lonely Hearts Club Band—medals included. It could have been that she planned to leave and didn't want to draw attention to herself. It could have been that her choice of clothing on that day was a coincidence, but I don't think that's the case."

"Even dressed plainly, someone with that much strawberry blond hair would have trouble escaping notice," Hadley said, "unless she concealed it somehow."

Drake nodded, his mouth set in a grim line. "We did get one report that someone had sighted a redhead at a truck stop the day after she disappeared, but the rest of the description didn't match up."

"So, over the years, there has been nothing, just *nothing?*" Hadley asked incredulously.

Drake shook his head ruefully. "I guess you could say that it gives a whole new meaning to the expression 'disappeared into thin air.' The stepfather hired a private investigator, but he didn't turn up anything, either. That was no surprise in more ways than one."

"What do you mean?"

"The PI was a virtual unknown with no track record of finding missing people."

"Couldn't the stepfather have afforded the best? Or, didn't he know any better?"

"You've hit upon one of the most interesting questions of this case."

Hadley experienced a sick feeling. "Could it have been that he didn't want to find her that badly?"

"I would hope not, but anything is possible."

She reached for the exhibit brochure from the back of the stroller. She looked again at the Van Gogh bedroom parody and the painting of the cowboy boots. The pictures seemed to be dots that her mind kept trying to connect.

A whimper interrupted her thoughts. Nicky had awakened and was trying to crawl out of his stroller. She lifted him out, along with his baby bag. Drowsily, he nestled his head against her shoulder. When she looked up, she found Drake studying them, his eyes murky. Before she could read the emotion in them, he glanced quickly away. In the awkward silence that followed, she took graham crackers and milk out of the bag for Nicky. But Nicky refused them. Instead, he extended his arms toward Drake.

"Let me have a shot of that," Drake said, pretending to take a swig from Nicky's two-handled cup. "Hey, that went down smooth." He handed the milk back to Nicky. "Come on, belly up to the bar."

Without protest, the toddler began to drink.

Hadley experienced a sinking feeling. There he was, hijacking her baby again—hijacking her whole life, giving her sexy looks all for naught. "Have you ever thought about joining the force in a place like Fairbanks or Honolulu?" she asked.

A glint of amusement appeared in his eyes. "Are you trying to get rid of me?"

"You like to fish, don't you? Alaskan salmon is a real treat."

"No, I've never considered Alaska. Besides, isn't there a shortage of women there?"

"What about Hawaii?" she asked, ignoring the question. "You could arrest people and work on your tan at the same time."

"Nope, I'm not going anywhere. I want to always be able to look out and see the peaks of the Rockies, to fish in mountain streams, to see wild horses kicking up dust on the plains. This is home. Always will be."

She sighed. Suddenly, Colorado seemed very small and crowded.

They watched in silence as Nicky, holding a half-eaten graham cracker, romped over tufts of bright green grass a few yards away. The lace on a sneaker came untied and started to whip in the air as he ran.

Hadley managed to grab him and hold him still just long enough to tie a firm double knot. As she set him down, a flash of illumination streaked across her mind.

She quickly turned. "Drake, remember that baby shoe sketch that Callie did?"

"Yes."

"I think I've seen the painting somewhere before."

His eyes narrowed. "What do you mean?"

"The sketch could have been the prototype for a painting that I remember. I'm almost certain."

CHAPTER NINE

"Where?" Drake rose to his feet.

"In one of the art galleries or museums I used to visit in Texas. I just can't remember which one."

"If you can't remember where, how can you be sure you remember the painting?" He was in full cop mode now, his gaze turning skeptical.

"Have you ever watched part of a movie before realizing you've seen it before?"

"Maybe."

"Have you ever heard a melody that you couldn't place, yet you knew you've heard it before?"

"I guess it's possible." His tone wasn't too convincing.

"At first, I just saw it for what it was—a sketch," she said. "It was more detailed than a typical outline for a painting. But the more I think about it in the context of her other work, the more familiar it looks."

Drake took a small ball from the stroller and tossed it at Nicky. "What do you mean?"

"Callie seemed to be in a Van Gogh phase. Van Gogh painted a lot of still lifes of shoes, probably more than any other famous artist. The shoes he painted were peasant shoes, shoes that showed someone's humble station in life. Callie did that with the boots and the baby shoes."

"Don't all artists try to copy the masters?" he asked. "I mean, isn't that how students learn?"

"Yes, but there's something else," she insisted. "The shoes in the painting had a message written on the laces."

"What kind of message?"

Nicky lobbed the ball back, striking Drake on the foot.

"It seemed like it had to do with animal extinction. It was an environmental statement, like the final extinct animal would be man."

"Couldn't it be just a coincidence? Callie wouldn't be the only artist with ideas like that. Somebody else could have done it."

"Maybe, but think about the globe with the headlines pasted on it. Think about the flowers in black and white. If you look at her more recent work as a whole, you can see that she liked to take objects or scenes that usually have a good association—like baby shoes—and give them a dark spin."

"I don't remember the baby shoe sketch having a written message," he said.

"There wasn't one, but look at the picture," she said, handing him the brochure. "Look how the laces are draped. That's the way it was in the painting, so the message would be visible."

Drake stroked his chin but said nothing.

"Don't you think it's worth checking out?"

He hesitated. Cops were such a hard sell. "I guess it wouldn't hurt."

"If I could just remember where I saw it."

"Do you remember when?"

"I went to a lot of galleries after Quint . . . I would go with friends. It helped keep me focused. All I know is that it was in Dallas or Austin and within the last three years or so. Austin, with the university and its youth culture, would appeal to someone like Callie. Yet Dallas is a place she could get lost in. I don't know. It was a strange time for me, Drake. I was in kind of a fog."

He slipped his arm around her shoulder and gave her a quick kiss on the temple. Her pulse jumped. Then just as casually, he released her. She struggled to get her mind back on track. "I have a friend who runs a gallery in Dallas," she said. "I can give her a call. Maybe she can help me place that painting."

"I can ask the local police to do it," he said.

Hadley hesitated. "I'm afraid they might treat this as some far-out notion or a wild goose chase. Would you first let me try to track it down on my own? I don't know anything about investigating, but I know something about art and that could make a difference."

"Go ahead. No harm in giving it a try."

"I hope you don't think I'm nuts," Hadley said.

"I've followed stranger leads."

"Did they pan out?"

"No."

Undaunted, Hadley grabbed Nicky and stuck him in his stroller. She loaded up his baby bag.

"Where are you going?" Drake asked.

"Home to get my camera. I'm going to take pictures of Callie's pieces, so I can send them to some people I know."

"There's no need to take Nicky," he said. "I'll take care of him until you get back."

She stopped. This wasn't what she had in mind. Her temple still tingled from his kiss. She didn't just need her camera, she needed to get away from him.

"I can't let you do that. I'm sure you have other plans."

"Nope, I'm free as a bird."

He grabbed the little ball from Nicky's stroller. In one deft move, he tossed it up, twirled it around and caught it behind his back. The little boy beamed with delight.

Drake tossed the ball back at Nicky. "How about another game, Slugger?"

"I'll be back in about fifteen minutes," Hadley said with resignation.

When Hadley returned with her camera and tripod, she saw that the bench on which they had been sitting was empty. The entire entourage, Drake, Nicky and stroller, was gone. She wandered through clusters of people gathered on the lawn until she spotted them by a concession stand. Nicky sat in his stroller eating a Popsicle. His t-shirt and a wide arc around his mouth were splotched with red. Drake, holding a bottle of water, leaned casually with one shoulder against a tree. His attentions were focused on a tall blonde with a smile bright enough to illuminate a closet. Hadley felt an unwanted constriction in her heart. If this wasn't a reminder of the man's overwhelming potential as a heartbreaker, she didn't know what was. As she approached, the corners of his mouth tipped into an awkward grin. "Hadley, I'd like for you to meet Brie Switzer. We just met. Brie, Hadley Spencer, Nicky's mom."

"It's nice to meet you," she said pleasantly.

"Hadley and I are old friends," Drake explained. "We bumped into each other today by accident."

Hadley knew the strategic value of that announcement. It shouldn't have mattered but it did. It was clear that Brie understood it, too. As she looked at Drake, her thickly lashed eyes brightened with interest. She wore a silky pink camisole that revealed a good inch of cleavage at the top and a peep of midriff at the bottom. Her long legs were encased in a pair of faded low-rise jeans. A short navy blue jacket completed the ensemble.

"Brie likes art, too," Drake said.

"Drake just told me some of the most interesting stuff about Van Gogh," she marveled. "He had a thing about shoes."

"Drake had a Van Gogh short course very recently," Hadley said dryly.

"Oh, really?" she replied with admiration.

Drake gave Hadley a look of warning.

"I'm looking for some artwork for my apartment," Brie went on. "I'm new in town."

"She runs a fitness studio," Drake explained. "In high school, she was a girls' track champion."

"Impressive," Hadley said. But what impressed her most was how much information Drake could extract from a woman in a matter of minutes. It appeared that police interrogation techniques had rather broad and varied applications.

"She's from the Oklahoma panhandle," he said. "Her parents have a wheat farm."

"America's breadbasket," Brie added with a giggle.

"I hope you'll like Mountain Spring," Hadley said.

"I think it's awesome," she said, glancing at Drake.

Hadley attempted to clean Nicky's face. At the same time, Brie bent over Nicky, revealing several more inches of cleavage. "Bye-bye, cutie pie."

Drake gave Nicky a pat on the arm. "Keep me posted, Hadley," he said. "See you later."

She walked back to the exhibit, sensing that was Drake's way of telling her that three was a crowd. She *had* wanted him to practice his charms where they would be better appreciated. So, why did her heart seem to be running in an opposite direction from her head?

She threw herself into the task at hand, painstakingly photographing the shoe sketch and a few other works. But thoughts of Drake kept intruding. If she were lucky, she told herself, Drake would follow Brie home like a lost puppy. When she finished, she stepped outside, hoping to find him gone, but there he was, standing at the foot of the steps, chatting with a school security guard. He spotted her almost instantly, as if he'd been watching for her. After giving the guard a cuff on the arm, he stepped up to help her with the stroller.

"I expected you to be gone," she said. "Brie was very charming. Maybe you can go jogging with her sometime."

"Hadley, she's just a kid—gorgeous and charming, all right, but a nineteen-year-old kid."

"So?"

"I'm going to try to fix her up with one of the rookies."

"That's nice." But she wasn't sure it would be all that nice for her.

Hadley's friend, Ursula Zapora, owned a small gallery in Dallas' art district. Hadley had sold several watercolors there and had long admired the older woman's keen understanding of art marketing and regional trends. She seemed to know almost every scenic artist in Texas who had ever touched a brush to canvas. Her support for local artists was generous and unfailing. When Quint died, she organized a benefit for children of officers killed in the line of duty. The proceeds went into a scholarship fund. It had been several months since she'd been in touch with Ursula. As usual, it was good to hear the sound of her slightly accented voice.

"When are you going to have some more watercolors for me?" she asked.

"Hopefully, later this year," Hadley said. "But I really called about something else, Ursula. I need your help in locating an artist."

Hadley described the baby shoe painting and told the story of the missing girl. "Do you remember seeing that sort of picture anywhere?"

"Not specifically. It's possible that if that was on exhibit anywhere in town, it could have been during one of my summer trips to Italy. Let me check around to see what I can find out."

"I'd really appreciate it."

"Any time, Sweetie."

"And, Ursula, please be discreet. I'm afraid that if it's Callie and she knows someone is looking for her, she might run."

"I understand. I'll approach it from the standpoint of an interested art connoisseur."

"Thanks. You're the best."

As soon as she hung up, Hadley began e-mailing the images to her, including the grainy picture of Callie from the newspaper. She hadn't expected instant answers from Ursula, but she realized that this could be much harder than she originally thought. All she had to go on was a sketch, a few pieces of artwork that demonstrated a certain style, and a hunch.

Days passed without a response, then a week. Hadley's hopes dissolved into a sense of foreboding. If the police couldn't find Callie, how could anyone else? In the meantime, she worked on the police car project, but without much success. It seemed she had the artistic equivalent of writer's block. Nothing she did looked right. She knew that the sooner she finished, the closer she would be to severing one tie to Drake. That would leave her with one final tie—Callie.

One afternoon, as she was disposing of another failed design by dragging it onto the computer's trash icon, the phone rang. It was Ursula.

"Hadley, I think I've found your painting—at least a record of it."

Her heart thumped. "You did? Where?"

"In Austin, at a gallery there. Marcel of Gallerie Marcel sold the painting, but he contacted the owner and compared it to the sketch. They're amazingly similar in composition. The shoes are the same, except that in the final piece, the laces have some sort of bleak environmental message written on them."

She shot up from her chair. "That's it," she said excitedly. "It has to be."

"There's still a bit of a problem," she cautioned.

"What do you mean?"

"The painting is signed by someone named Sarah Reed."

Hadley sat back down. Her mind spun with disappointment, then slowly rebounded. "Callie was a runaway," she said. "It would have been logical for her to assume a new identity. That would explain why she has been so hard to track."

"Hadley, she doesn't fit the physical description either."

"You sent him the picture?"

"Yes, but he says Sarah Reed has very short blond hair, almost as short as a boy's. She also wears glasses."

Hadley paused to regain her footing. "Maybe it's a disguise."

"Maybe. He said there were some facial similarities, but he couldn't be sure."

"Does the gallery owner know where she is now?" Hadley persisted.

"No," Ursula said. "He hasn't seen her in months. She used to bring in paintings regularly. He said he sold several over the last couple of years. He tried to call her but the number in his files is no longer valid."

Hadley's heart sank again. If it was Callie, was she still on the run?

"He said she has exhibited in a number of places around town, including the university museum," Ursula added.

Hadley imagined the painting at the university and it seemed to fit perfectly.

"The museum director there is an old friend of mine," Ursula said, "but he won't be back in the office until tomorrow. In the meantime, I wanted to give you an update."

Hadley thanked her, then hung up, her heart racing. She was

at once hopeful and fearful. Part of her wanted to run to Callie's mother, but she didn't dare. She knew that hopes lifted, then dashed delivered the cruelest disappointment of all.

The phone rang numerous times the following morning, but the callers were all clients, except for one very persistent carpet-cleaning salesman who wouldn't take "I have no wall-to-wall carpet" for an answer. Each time, she grabbed it on the first ring, only to be disappointed. After lunch, it rang again. This time, it was Ursula.

"Hadley, I may have found your girl."

Her heart leaped to her throat. "Where?"

"In Austin. She works in a bookstore during the week and in a natural foods store on weekends. She's an artist the rest of the time, in addition to squeezing in a university art course once in a while. My friend at the museum remembers the shoe painting. He also described her as someone of extraordinary versatility."

"That sounds just like Callie," she said excitedly. "Did he think she was the same girl as the one in the newspaper picture?"

"He said it's possible, but he can't say for certain. Hadley, I went ahead and gave him a few more details, but he can be trusted. I emphasized that if this is the right girl, she has done nothing illegal. She's just the subject of a missing persons report."

Hadley took a deep breath infused with hope. "I know some of the things don't add up, but the sketch and the matching baby shoe painting have to mean something. There can be no other explanation for it unless . . ." Hadley had been hesitant to consider the possibility, but she could no longer avoid it. "Unless," she continued, "the painting could be some sort of copycat."

"Let's hope not," Ursula said, "because this is a sad story in need of a happy ending."

When Hadley called Drake to tell him she had some news, he insisted on driving over. He'd just completed a training exercise in the area. In addition, the commander had given him more material to pass on in regard to the police design project.

He appeared on her front porch late that afternoon, wearing a SWAT team t-shirt and cargo-style trousers. A revolver was strapped to his hip. He looked more handsome than ever, if that were possible, and Hadley hated that.

"I got away as quickly as I could," he said, handing her a design folder. The instant he stepped inside, Nicky's face lit up like sunshine and he made a beeline for him. The string under his chin barely kept his red cowboy hat from flying off his head.

In one smooth and seemingly effortless motion, Drake swooped up the boy.

"Drake, I found someone who might be Callie."

His gaze shot to hers like an arrow. "Where?"

"In Austin, Texas."

He set Nicky on his feet and the boy toddled off toward a small box of toys on the living room rug.

"What makes you think it could be her?"

Hadley told him how the sketch closely matched the painting and about the similarity in the ages of Callie and Sarah Reed.

"Even their artistic strengths were described as similar," she added. As they sat on the sofa, Drake listened with what she imagined to be the ingrained skepticism that came with a cop's job. When she finished, he sat silently for a moment, his face a mask of concentration.

Hadley felt a creeping apprehension. "You don't think it's her?"

"I don't know, but it's a lead—the first in a long time."

"What do we do now?"

"The only way to identify this girl is to do a little more digging, then question her," he said. "That's where it gets a little tricky."

"What do you mean?"

"If it is Callie and an officer is sent after her, she could panic and take off."

"What do police do in a case like that?"

"Sometimes you have to get creative," he said. "But first things first. We need to try to confirm the ID. There are various databases we can search."

Hadley handed Drake a slip of paper on which she had already written the names, numbers and e-mail addresses of her contacts. As he stuck it in his pocket, Nicky walked up and dropped a copy of *Pinocchio* in his lap. With his hat resting on his back, the boy crawled up beside him and clumsily pried it open. Then he looked up at Drake as a cue to start reading.

"Nicky, we'll read later," Hadley said gently. "Drake and I have to talk right now."

"Hold on, Cowboy," Drake said, patting him on the knee. Nicky settled beside him, apparently satisfied.

"It would be wonderful if that was Callie, wouldn't it?" Hadley asked.

"Yes, but try not to get your hopes up too high."

"I won't." She understood his skepticism, but it was more than she had expected. He looked at her a moment with that penetrating gray gaze that always sent a surge of unwanted longing all the way down to the soles of her shoes.

"Good work, Hadley."

Her heart lifted. "Thanks."

He turned to the book and began to read. His voice filled with inflection, filled the room. Nicky rested his head against Drake's arm just as he did when she read to him. Her heart twisted. She'd always be there for Nicky. Little did he know that Drake wouldn't be.

The following weekend, Hadley was having a late breakfast of homemade cinnamon muffins. They had been Quint's favorite, a Saturday morning ritual to which she had returned. She had been holding fast to memories these days. They helped chase away thoughts of Drake. She was pouring herself a second cup of tea when the phone rang. Her heartbeat quickened at the unexpected sound of his voice on the other end.

"Hadley, I'm here in town at the police station. I have some news."

"Good or bad?"

"Can I come over?"

She felt a twinge of anxiety. "I'll be waiting for you."

She wanted desperately for a successful end to this case not only to end a mother's heartbreak, but to prevent her own. When her official dealings with him were over, she could get back her life, her simple, unencumbered and safe life.

He was there within a half hour, wearing a Saturday-morning stubble and his standard off-duty uniform of jeans and a sweater. As usual, Nicky rushed to greet him.

This can't stop soon enough, Hadley thought. *I can't let Nicky get too close to him.* But she knew in her heart that it was already too late. The only salvation was that two-year-olds were equipped with short memories and resilient hearts.

"Something smells terrific," he said.

"Come in the kitchen."

With a hauntingly bittersweet feeling, she handed Drake two muffins on a piece of her mismatched blue and white china. She poured coffee for both of them while Nicky sat on his booster seat with a muffin half.

"The local police may have a positive ID," Drake announced.

148

"Indications are that it's Callie."

The elation that went through her was almost electric. "That's wonderful. What makes them think it's her?"

"Driver's license registration, basically. Even though she uses the name Sarah Reed, she listed the same birthplace and date of birth as Callie Murphy."

"How could it not be her?" she asked excitedly. "The coincidences are just too startling."

"They're significant all right," he said. "There was also a Social Security number, but they didn't have anything to compare it to," he continued. "At the time Callie disappeared, she hadn't yet applied for a card, which was pretty unusual. But Callie was never a girl to operate within the confines of convention."

"What are you going to do now?" she asked.

"I've got an idea, but I could use your help."

"What do you mean?"

"Given the turnover in the Mountain Spring Police Department since Callie disappeared, I'm the only one around who has had any face-to-face contact with her. That makes me the logical one to attempt a positive identification. Once she recognizes me, though, she might head for the exits."

"What about her mother?"

"I'd like to confirm that this is Callie before we contact Mrs. Murphy. I don't want to get her hopes up and then have them crashing down. This is where an intermediary would be helpful. What I'm saying is: I'd like to fly down to Austin. I'd like for you to go with me."

Her heart thumped. "Me, an intermediary? I've never done anything like that before. What if I make a mistake and ruin everything?"

"You won't. Just be natural. Be your sweet, charming self."

There he went again, playing the opposite sex out of force of habit. "What do you want me to do?"

"We'll go into the store where she works and I'll discreetly try to make an identification. Once that's done, you can approach her as a fellow artist who admires her work and take it from there. We'll work out the details later. The object is to identify her and let her mother know she's OK. It's not to force her back home against her will. We need to stress that above all."

Hadley swallowed hard. She was nervous just thinking about it. And the last thing she needed was to spend more time with Drake. But after seeing the dull, lingering pain in Mrs. Murphy's eyes, how could she say no? She took a deep breath. "I'll get Aunt Margaret to stay with Nicky."

"No need for that," he said.

She looked at him in surprise. "Isn't he kind of young to be out on police business?"

"Not in this case."

"What do you mean?"

"He'll help create a non-threatening atmosphere. What's less intimidating than a mother and a baby?"

CHAPTER TEN

Mother Earth's Natural Foods was a half hour from the airport on a normal day, but today road construction had slowed traffic to a crawl. Drake eased the rental car past a maze of flagmen and orange cones.

Hadley sat quietly, her mind jumping from one time frame to another. The trip had stirred up a whirlwind of emotions. She'd known it wouldn't be easy to come back to Texas. Austin was one thing, with its relatively pleasant memories. Dallas was another. When the plane had begun its descent over the haze-shrouded Dallas skyline, she'd turned away from the window.

As she did, she'd felt the warmth of Drake's hand on hers. It was as if he'd read her mind. "I'm sorry about the stopover here," he'd said. "It couldn't be avoided."

Nicky had been a little trooper, thanks in part to Drake who had read him the funnies and made him a hat out of a piece of newspaper.

"Nervous?" he asked.

"A little," she admitted.

"A touch of adrenalin can be a good thing. It sharpens your senses."

Like the thorough officer that he was, Drake had taken care of the preliminaries. He'd made sure that Callie would be on duty that day. He had also brought along her telephone number and home address, plus a map showing how to get there. He'd coached Hadley on what to do. She couldn't let him down.

They found the store in a Spanish-style building in an older part of Austin. The tile roof was terra cotta speckled with blue and gray. The stucco walls were a sun-bleached tan. Taped to the plate glass windows were notices of the specials of the day—fresh tofu, four-fruit granola in bulk, and herbal teas.

"Look, Drake," she pointed out. "The lettering on those signs . . . It's something like an artist would do."

He lowered his sunglasses for a moment to get a better view, then turned into the store's parking lot. He switched off the engine and turned to Hadley.

"Ready to do some shopping?" His tone was surprisingly light.

She nodded, her pulse rate picking up.

"Let's see if we can get our girl."

Drake extricated Nicky from the child seat that Hadley had lugged along. She fell into step beside Drake as he carried him into the store.

Inside, they were immediately surrounded by the yeasty aroma of the bread of the day—oatmeal wheat. Old-fashioned light fixtures threw a warm, golden glow over mounds of organically raised produce. Bins of whole grains lined a wall. A sign hanging from the ceiling drew attention to a coffee bar, featuring fair-trade coffee beans.

Her heart strumming, Hadley placed Nicky into a grocery cart and glanced around the store. At one register stood a young man with a ponytail who was ringing up purchases for a woman with two children. The other register was occupied by a middle-aged woman.

Hadley, who saw no one remotely resembling Callie's description, felt a pang of concern. She glanced at Drake. She could tell by his attentive posture that behind his dark lenses, he was sizing up the store as though it were a crime scene.

Suddenly, a door marked "Employees Only" swung open.

Pushing a cart filled with potatoes was a young woman with retro, cats-eye glasses and short, blond hair. Hadley's pulse leapt like a drop of water on a hot skillet.

"Let's go take a look," Drake said calmly.

As the girl began restocking the potato bin, Drake stepped behind a nearby display while Hadley strolled toward her. The girl glanced up, revealing an attractive heart-shaped face. She wore jeans, and what appeared to be a World War II–vintage white rayon blouse with padded shoulders.

"Hi. Are you finding everything OK?" she asked.

"Do you have any raw cashews?" Hadley asked.

"Two aisles over," she said.

Her heart racing, Hadley proceeded. When she got to the aisle, Drake was already there.

"It's her," he whispered.

"You're sure?" she said.

"No doubt."

There was a fluttering inside her chest that was part elation, part trepidation.

"I'll stay here," he said with an encouraging smile. "You'll do fine. Don't worry."

She was just a few steps away when he called her back. "You forgot something." He tossed the package of cashews into her cart. Hadley smiled back at him nervously as he gave her a thumb's up.

She took a deep breath before returning to the produce section. "Where are these potatoes grown?" Hadley asked.

"In the Rio Grande Valley. We should start getting locally grown produce within a few months."

"Pardon me, but aren't you Sarah Reed, the artist?"

The girl looked at her in surprise. Hadley noticed a faint sprinkling of freckles across her nose. "Yes, how did you know?"

"Someone at the museum told me you worked here. I'm an

admirer of your work."

"You are? Thank you."

"Actually, I stumbled onto your work in a very unusual way. If you could manage a few moments of free time, could we talk privately? I'd like to tell you about it."

The expression in her green eyes turned slightly wary. She looked at her watch. "I have a break coming up, but I can take it a little early. Let me tell the manager."

In a few moments, she was back. She led Hadley to the employee canteen. Hadley parked the cart by the door, and lifted Nicky out. Inside the canteen was a small, round table with four chairs.

"Have a seat," the girl said. "Do you drink coffee? I can get us something from the coffee bar."

"That would be nice," she replied, trying to appear relaxed.

"Any preference? Cappuccino, latte, espresso? If you'd rather, we have herbal teas." Her voice had a bit of a husky quality to it that seemed to say, "If you push me, I'll push back."

"Whatever you're having will be fine."

Nicky's soft and warm presence soothed Hadley as she waited and reminded her why she was there: to bring a mother and child back together.

The girl returned a few moments later with two cappuccinos and a small carton of vanilla soymilk for Nicky. "Is it all right for him to have this?" she asked.

"Yes, thanks." She was touched by the consideration shown to a toddler by this reputably prickly girl.

Gingerly, the girl took a sip of her coffee. "What is it you wanted to tell me?"

Hadley shifted Nicky on her lap. Her coffee was still untouched. "I'm an artist, too," she began, "although I'm not nearly as talented as you are. I enjoy going to exhibits and when I see something that strikes me, it usually stays in my mind.

Your baby shoe picture was one of those. It had additional impact because I was pregnant at the time."

"Thank you, but if you want to buy it, I'm afraid it's been sold."

"That's what I heard. Congratulations. But there's something else that led me to seek you out. Not long ago, I saw a sketch that could have been the basis for that painting."

Her spine straightened. "Where?"

"At an exhibit at Mountain Spring High School. The show was dedicated to a missing girl named Callie Murphy. It was her sketch. It could well have been yours."

Hadley's announcement seemed to extinguish all light from the girl's eyes. "What are you talking about? I don't know any Callie Whatever."

Hadley's heartbeat quickened as she pressed the issue further. "The sketch and the painting are virtually identical in composition. It's too much of a coincidence, unless, maybe, the sketch is the work of a copycat."

"It has to be." Her voice was constricted.

"The puzzling thing is that both were apparently done the same year—the sketch in Colorado, the painting in Texas."

The girl reacted with a frozen stare.

"Callie's mother still lives in Mountain Spring," Hadley said. "She's endured a lot of pain during the last five years."

"Why are you telling me all this?" she cried. "I'm Sarah Reed."

Hadley persisted gently. "Callie's teacher said that she was the most talented student she'd ever had."

The girl set down her coffee cup with a thump, causing the contents to splash on the table. "How many times do I have to tell you that I'm not Callie Murphy?"

"There's something Callie may not know," Hadley continued

calmly. "Her mother divorced her stepfather after she left. He's dead now."

The girl's eyes showed a flash of surprise before she broke into tears. She took off her glasses.

Hadley got up and put her hand on her shoulder. "It's all right, Callie."

Nicky, who was perched on Hadley's hip, patted the girl's head as if she were a puppy. Close-up, Hadley could see the strawberry blond roots of her hair.

Callie looked up and managed a tearful smile for the little boy.

"It would mean a lot to your mother if she could see you again."

The girl's expression hardened. She wiped her eyes with the backs of her hands. "No, I'm not going home—not after what she did to me."

Hadley swallowed hard. Whatever it was, she knew not to ask. She'd already pressed the girl to her limit. "Callie, we're going to have to report that you've been found," she explained gently. "We can't withhold information from the police about an open case."

"Who's 'we'?"

"A friend came with me—Drake Matthieson."

"You came here with a cop? Is this some kind of a trap? He can't arrest me. I haven't done anything wrong." Her voice was edged with alarm.

"No, Callie, you haven't done anything wrong. No one can make you go back to Mountain Spring if you don't want to. I promise."

Callie's eyes remained narrow with mistrust.

"Drake is on the police force in Denver now," Hadley explained. "He no longer has jurisdiction on this case. He's here as a civilian—as someone who never stopped caring what happened to you."

"Yeah, I bet," she retorted cynically.

"Honest," Hadley said. "You can ask him yourself."

"Just tell 'Officer Hottie' I'm not going home."

"Who?"

" 'Officer Hottie.' That's what they called him."

She sighed inwardly. Why should she be surprised that he'd have a nickname like that?

"I'll relay your message to 'Officer Hottie.' Is there anything you want me to tell your mother?"

"No. I've already told you I don't want to see her."

"All right," she said with a twist of sadness.

The girl looked up. Her eyes were shining with unshed tears. "I can't believe that you found me through that sketch."

"That shows something about the power of your work," Hadley said. "We pursued it to the point where we found out that Sarah Reed's birthplace and date matched that of Callie Murphy."

Suddenly looking very tired, the girl dropped her head into her hands. "I can't believe this," she muttered again. "I should have known better."

"Callie, I'm sorry. I truly admire your work and I couldn't help but be affected by the fact you were missing. I know I'm an intruder in the new life you have built for yourself, but please try to look at it this way: Knowing that you're alive and well will mean so much to so many people."

"Yeah, hoards of 'em," she said, raising her head. "I can count 'em on one finger—my art teacher."

"There's Drake. If he didn't care, he would have forgotten about you when he left Mountain Spring. It would really please him if you could step out for a moment and say hello. Your case has been bothering him for a long time."

"This had better not be some kind of a trick."

"Of course not. Remember what I said. Even if he had jurisdiction in this case, he wouldn't have anything to arrest you for. If you don't believe me, ask him."

She stared at the wall for a moment without moving. Then she wiped her eyes, put her glasses back on and got up slowly. Hadley opened the door and found Drake standing restlessly by a pile of pomegranates. He straightened at the sight of her.

"Drake, say hello to Callie."

He grinned crookedly, betraying his normal reserve. "Hey," he said.

"Hey," she said nervously. "She promised you couldn't arrest me or anything. She said I didn't have to go home if I didn't want to. She'd better be right, or nothing's going to stand between me and that door."

"She's right," he said.

"You can't even get me for tearing up that speeding ticket that you gave me?"

He shook his head. "Your mother paid it long ago."

A crimp appeared at the corner of her mouth.

"Callie, it's really great to see you again, to know you're OK."

She shrugged.

"Remember Ben, the skinny kid with the crush on you?"

She nodded.

"He asked about you. He's an Army sergeant now."

A raised brow hinted at surprise. "He was like me—kind of misunderstood."

Drake nodded. "We can talk sometime if you like."

She shook her head firmly. "I've already told her everything I'm going to say."

"Suit yourself."

A moment of silence followed.

"You know," she said finally, "I have every right to be mad at you guys. But I guess you're just trying to help. For whatever it's worth, I'm fine. Now, I just want to be left alone."

Drake handed her a business card and held out his hand. "Bye, Callie. Call if you need anything."

Haltingly, she slipped her palm in his. "Thanks, but I doubt if I will."

Hadley handed Nicky over to Drake and embraced the girl. Callie's stiffened body yielded. "All the best to you, Callie."

The girl stepped over and patted Nicky on the back. Then she looked at both of them again. "You two aren't, you know, married or something, are you?"

"No," Drake said quickly.

An awkward pause followed. "I have to get back to work," Callie said, suddenly sounding very tired.

She looked at Hadley once more with a warning flashing in her eyes. "About my mom. Don't forget what I said. I mean it."

It was well after midnight when they arrived back in Mountain Spring. Drake carried a sleeping Nicky inside the house.

He had insisted on following her home. She'd insisted he didn't. He'd won by rattling off statistics about nighttime crime's peak hours.

"I'll make some coffee," she said after she'd put Nicky to bed. "It will keep you alert on the way home."

He argued that she shouldn't put herself to the trouble. This time, she prevailed.

When she returned to the living room with a tray of coffee and some homemade cookies, she found Drake lying on the sofa. One long leg dangled off. His eyes were closed and the slow rhythm of his breathing told her that he was asleep.

Quietly, she set down the tray and sat on the edge of the coffee table. She looked at the square lines of his jaw, the way his lips parted slightly and her heart constricted. She had an overwhelming urge to lean over and kiss his forehead like she did Nicky's, but she didn't dare. For a man who was so good at keeping his relationships with women superficial, he was such a sucker for kids. Even Callie's lingering defiance hadn't seemed to ruffle him. He seemed to know when to nudge, when to step back, and when to pull out the right bag of tricks for the occasion. How could a woman not fall for a man like that?

Frightened by her own thoughts, she jumped up suddenly, nearly upending the tray with a careless sweep of her wrist. She grabbed it just as one coffee mug slid into the other with a loud, glassy clink.

Drake sat straight up.

"I'm sorry," Hadley apologized, mopping up spilled coffee with a napkin. "I almost knocked over the tray."

He put his hands over his face and let them down slowly. "I fell asleep, didn't I?"

"Just for a minute."

"I laid down for a moment to ponder what Callie's mother might have done to her."

"I've been wondering about it, too," Hadley said. "It sounds like something more than a badly timed marriage to the wrong man. I thought that learning about her stepfather would make a difference."

"That wasn't the trump card I'd hoped, either."

Hadley went to the kitchen and brought back fresh mugs of coffee. She sat at the opposite end of the sofa.

"I'll notify the local police the first thing in the morning that Callie has been found," Drake said "They'll call Mrs. Murphy, but I'm sure she'll want every detail she can get from you."

"Of course. I'm just sorry that not all the news will be good."

"There's no way to make Callie come home," he said. "She's of legal age now and has no outstanding warrants. At least after five years Mrs. Murphy will finally know that her daughter is OK."

"It's not over yet," Hadley said. "I believe in the healing power of time, Drake."

He looked at her a moment, gulped down the rest of his coffee, then got up. "It's late. I need to go." He reached for her hand and pulled her up with him. He led her to the door, then turned toward her. "I want to thank you for what you did. You're the one who found Callie."

"I couldn't have done it by myself."

"Without you, she might not have been found."

"Maybe it was pure, dumb luck," she said. "Maybe it was just meant to be."

He slipped his arms around her and gave her a brotherly kiss on the forehead. The softness of his lips against her skin made her blood dance. "I can't thank you enough," he said. "There are no maybes about that."

He kissed her again, this time on the cheekbone. It was as if she were having a dream in which she wanted to flee, but her feet were stuck to the ground. She was powerless to move as his lips traced a delicate path down her cheek until they touched her mouth.

At first, the kiss was hardly more than a whisper, a tease, a nibble. Then suddenly, his lips came down on hers with need, hunger and conviction. Her heart pounded wildly in her chest as she melted in his embrace. Then abruptly, he released her, leaving her dizzy.

"Before, I apologized when I kissed you," he said, his eyes murky. "This time, I'm not the least bit sorry."

In a parting gesture, he touched her shoulder, and strode out the door.

She wasn't sorry, either. The next morning, she spent a good deal of time brooding about it. He'd kissed her like a man who could write the definitive manual on the art of kissing. She was mad at herself for letting it happen.

She knew that something more powerful than she was had overcome her. He had awakened in her an inner need that she thought had died with Quint. And that left her vulnerable. Worst of all, he'd kissed her as though he meant it.

She went to her screened back porch and gathered up her gardening tools for some cathartic yard work, but before she could step outside, her phone rang. She'd been expecting it to. The handset was in her pocket.

The voice at the other end of the line was tearful. It belonged to Mrs. Murphy.

"The police just called," she sobbed. "They said you found my little girl."

Hadley's heart lifted. "Yes, we found her."

"I'm so grateful. I want to know everything, everything you can tell me."

Within minutes, Mrs. Murphy was at the door. The powder on her face was streaked with tears.

She greeted Hadley with a hug. "You don't know how much this means to me. If only . . ." It was a sentence that needed no ending. "Thank goodness at least, that she's all right."

As they sat on the sofa, drinking herbal tea, Hadley told her in painstaking detail about Callie. But no matter how much information she gave, Mrs. Murphy wanted more: Did she look healthy? Was she thin? How did she sound?

"The police said she doesn't want to see me. She can't really mean that, can she? Not after all this time." She stared at Hadley with a tortured expression, as if she were begging her to say it wasn't so.

Hadley placed a hand over Mrs. Murphy's. It felt cold. "That's what she claimed," she said gently, "but that doesn't mean she won't change her mind someday."

"Exactly how did she say it?"

Hadley swallowed hard. There was no way to lighten the load of Callie's words. "She said, 'I don't want to see her again, not after what she did to me.' "

Mrs. Murphy broke into sobs. Nicky, who had been playing on the floor, looked up.

"I'm sorry," Hadley said helplessly. "We thought that since her stepfather is gone there would be nothing to keep her from coming home."

Mrs. Murphy struggled to regain her composure. She dabbed at her eyes with a tissue. "She's entitled to feel the way she does because I also did her wrong."

Hadley looked at her in surprise. "What do you mean?"

The woman took a deep breath. Suddenly, she looked pale and tired, older than her years. "There are some things I never told the police. I couldn't. My husband threatened to make my daughter look bad if I did." Hadley noticed her hands were trembling.

"Callie told me that when her stepfather had too much to drink, he made advances toward her. She wasn't telling the truth much in those days, so I didn't believe her. I'd already caught her lying about her whereabouts a few times. I thought she was making up lies about her stepfather to get back at me for remarrying so soon. As it turned out, she was telling me the truth."

"How did you find out?" Hadley asked.

"He admitted it to me before he died." She twisted the tissue in her lap. "Callie must have thought I cared more about him than her. In hindsight, I can't blame her for feeling the way she did."

At a loss for words, Hadley touched Mrs. Murphy's sleeve instead.

"You see, after Callie's father died, I had no money," the woman continued. "The medical expenses had wiped us out. When a friend introduced me to Stuart, he seemed like a godsend. He had financial security to offer and he was nice to Callie. Although Callie didn't take to the marriage too well, I thought everything would eventually work out. Her stepfather brought home that little convertible for her from the family car dealership. We had a nice house. I thought she'd be happy, but she never adjusted. Instead, she got rebellious.

"When she ran away, the police asked Stuart some pretty hard questions. In turn, he went after that poor boy, Ben. Finally, he started drinking so much that I couldn't stay with him any longer. I just left. Although I was entitled to, I didn't take a dime of his money."

She blotted the tears from her eyes. "So, that's the story. I guess I can't blame Callie for still not wanting to see me."

"I'm so sorry," Hadley said. There seemed to be nothing else to say.

Drake listened without a hint of surprise as Hadley retold the story that evening. It was as if he'd known it all along.

"We suspected as much, but we couldn't verify it without being able to talk to Callie."

"You did everything you could. We all did."

"Don't sell yourself short, Hadley," he said. "You were terrific. There's something about you that makes people let their guard down."

At the moment, she was struggling mightily to keep her own guard up. She couldn't look at him without thinking of what it was like to be in his arms.

"Thanks again for everything," he said.

"You didn't need to drive all the way down just to say thanks again."

A brief pause followed. "I came because there's something I want to tell you."

She stared at him. "What is it?"

"I've been doing some thinking. I've decided to get back into the dating circuit."

Her heart took a leap upward, and then went crashing down like a fledgling trying out its wings.

"You and I have been spending a lot of time together and maybe that's not such a good thing—for either one of us."

She nodded. She knew he was right, but she didn't trust her voice enough to say yes. Doing that would risk betraying what was in her heart.

"We can still be friends—all of us, you, me and Nicky."

"Sure," she said, feigning indifference.

"I'll still be available to replace a light switch or nail on a shingle."

In exchange, she offered something she was sure he'd never need again. "I'll still be your art consultant," she joked weakly.

He glanced at the ceiling as if he were mulling over the idea. "You're serious about that?"

She looked at him with alarm. "What do you mean?"

"Since you mentioned it, I could use some advice."

"About what?"

"About fixing up my apartment," he said. "It would be nice to come home to a place that's bright and cozy, not smelling of stale pepperoni and dark enough to grow mushrooms. You know, the kind of place I could bring a woman to."

Hadley blinked. "Who?"

"No one in particular. There are plenty of women out there. No need to limit myself."

She stared at him, unable to speak. Just how resistant to commitment could a man be? On the other hand, why did it even matter to her? Yet it did, and her blood churned with something she couldn't define.

"Would you help me?" he asked. "You don't have to do any actual work. I'd just appreciate your advice on getting the place into shape."

She swallowed hard. "Surely among harems past is a decorator."

"I've already asked. She's married and eight and a half months pregnant. With twins."

Hadley frowned.

"Hadley, you're the only woman I've seen in the last year. And you're great at this sort of thing."

Her mind scrambled. If she refused, it might reveal that she cared more about him than he cared about her. That was an indignity she didn't need.

If she accepted, it could give him the opposite impression. She'd plump a few pillows—if he had any—and send him back to Bachelor Land with a show of total support. She'd wish him good luck. She'd be a real pal. And she'd be doing herself a huge favor. She put on a game face.

"Just say when."

CHAPTER ELEVEN

Drake's apartment was located on the outskirts of Denver in an area of themed apartment complexes. It was a place where everyone seemed to be just passing through. Missing were the tree-lined streets, multi-paned windows and ivy-covered brick that were the basic requirements for anything Hadley would call home.

The complex was called Kensington Row, but nothing seemed to suggest anything English other than the fact the tiny patch of turf in front of it was soggy from a recent shower. It was ordinary beige brick with plain windows. The tiny balconies were barren except for an occasional patio set or hanging plant.

Hadley parked in an area marked "guests" and took a few deep breaths in a futile attempt to settle her anxiety. Suddenly, Drake appeared through her windshield, heading straight toward her in an athletic gait. His hands were in the pockets of a pair of gray gym shorts that showed off well-muscled and nicely shaped legs. He wore a black sweatshirt pushed up to the elbows and running shoes. A white towel was hooked around his neck.

Redecorating his apartment? He must be kidding, she thought ruefully. A man who looked like that could have purple walls and a pet python and a good number of women wouldn't care.

Hadley got out of the car.

"I was watching for you," he said, flashing a white grin. "Let me show you in."

If this had been his car-side manner as a patrolman, a woman might have let him throw the book at her.

"Thank you," she said stiffly to mask the effect he was having on her. She was almost sorry she'd come, but how could she refuse him just one more favor after all he'd done for her and Nicky? She'd fulfill this request quickly and efficiently. She'd go home and work madly on the car design project. Then it would be over and perhaps she could at last quell the stirrings within her heart.

Drake unbuckled Nicky from the back seat and hoisted the boy up on his shoulders. It was with a sense of irony that she noted the ease at which he had picked up on the rhythm of their lives. Hadley followed them up two short flights of stairs to a second-floor apartment. A pair of military-style boots sat on the doormat. Not that she needed a gritty reminder of the work that he loved above all else.

He took Nicky down from his shoulders and opened the door. When he stepped aside to allow her to enter, he touched her elbow, setting off a shower of emotional sparks within her. It took a moment before she could focus on the task at hand.

The plainness of the apartment struck her first. The dingy white walls were bare except for a crooked row of commendation plaques. The blinds were haphazardly drawn up at varying levels.

What looked like a heap of newspapers and magazines teetering on four legs was a small dining table. A bulletproof vest hung on the back of one chair. The other chair was wreathed in a fine layer of dust.

"What do you think?" he asked cheerfully.

Hadley pressed a finger under her nose to avoid sneezing. "I already have a few suggestions."

"Take your time and look around. I'll keep an eye on Nicky."

Hadley took a few steps into the living room. The tweedy brown sofa was without adornment except for a pillow from the bed and a dirty white sock peeping out from under one of the cushions. The matching chair was a repository for a briefcase and a jumble of papers. On an end table was a dead cactus. The television rested on the box in which it had been shipped. An assortment of paperback books sat in bookcases fashioned from plastic crates. It all added up to an unsettled, just-a-place-to-sleep look. It was. His real home was the police station. With trepidation, she continued into a small kitchen. It was surprisingly clean but bare except for a coffee maker and a well-worn catcher's mitt that hung on a peg.

"You use your kitchen to store sports equipment?"

"That's my oven mitt," he said, looking slightly affronted.

"You don't cook much, do you?"

His mouth twisted slightly. "Not since the great balcony fire of 2004. I ruined a good jacket putting it out, along with a seven-dollar T-bone."

Hadley looked at the list of carryout restaurants posted on the refrigerator and almost felt sorry for him.

"Come on, and I'll show you the bedroom."

She braced herself.

It didn't say "home sweet home" either. The bed was covered with a ribbed brown spread, which barely concealed a pair of jeans that appeared to have been kicked under the hem. One pillow was missing. On a nightstand was a copy of a suspense novel. Near a window was a ski-style exercise machine. Hadley turned to find a dresser and chest of drawers. The chest was bare. On the dresser was an eight-by-ten portrait that stopped her in her tracks. Pictured were a handsome couple, a man with Drake's strong jaw and a woman with a wealth of dark, shoulder-length hair. There was an adolescent boy, sturdy and handsome and with a familiar gray gaze. His eyes had a long-gone look of innocence. Next to him stood a younger boy with his father's light brown hair. Then there was a girl of about eight with a new-toothed smile, taffy-colored hair and lovely pale eyes. Hadley's heart constricted.

She lifted the heavy silver frame. Its footprint was visible in the dust. "You were a beautiful family."

"Thank you. The picture was taken a few months before the accident."

Hadley ached for all of them.

"Now, what were those suggestions you had?" he asked, quickly changing the subject.

Hadley stepped back into the living room and sneezed. "You might think about doing some dusting."

"I'll see what I can do. But what I really want is for this place to look a little more inviting—like your house."

He was going to woo women in a room with her imprint. That had been the whole idea, but suddenly it didn't seem quite fair.

"Is imitation not the sincerest form of flattery?" he asked.

"Maybe. Well, where do I start?"

Hadley raised the living room blinds as high as they would go and took another look. The added light revealed a stray sneaker under the coffee table and a pocket-sized red book on an end table. Hadley swallowed hard. This had to be the infamous "G file." She was trying to pretend it wasn't there until Nicky grabbed it. Snatching it out of his hand, she gave it to Drake.

"You really should be more careful with your valuables," she said.

A wry grin crossed his face as he popped the book into the pocket of his shorts. Nicky whimpered.

"It's OK, little guy," he said. "They're too old for you anyway."

Hadley sighed.

"As you were saying—about the apartment."

She took a few seconds to gather her wits. "I'd start with

some color," she said finally. "Almost everything you have is brown. Get some pillows for the sofa. It doesn't matter if they match as long as they have the same dominant colors. A rug or two would help break up the monotony of the carpet. Can you paint the walls?"

"I think so, as long as I paint them white again before I move out—which I don't plan to do anytime soon."

"Color can warm up a room and give it a cozy feel, depending on which one you choose."

"How about green—like yours?"

Hadley blinked. "Well, I guess that would work, but I think a muted gold or beige would go better with the furniture. Get some pictures for the walls—something restful like nature scenes. You could even get some textiles like Navaho-style blankets. Get some candles and some plants. And don't forget to water them. File away the magazines."

"And the bedroom?" he asked.

She noted a mischievous twinkle in his eyes. "Shouldn't you consult 'Playboy' on that one?"

"The Contemporary Debauchery look wasn't what I had in mind."

"What do you have in mind?"

He folded his arms across his chest and studied her with interest. "I want to know what you think. That's why I asked you to come over."

Her cheeks warmed slightly. "You need more pillows. Try some sheets in mixed, bright colors. She ticked off the answer to his question as if he were a graphic design client. But not far below the surface of a calm and professional exterior, her emotions churned. It was as if she were standing too close to a fire.

"If that's all, I think I should be going now," she said abruptly. She grabbed Nicky who was attempting to scale Drake's coffee table. It had several white coffee cup rings on it.

"But you just got here."

"This is enough to get you started."

He looked mildly chagrined. "Well, thanks for the advice. I'll go to the paint store tomorrow."

She turned to go.

"Hadley," he said softly.

She turned back to face him.

"I just wanted to tell you I'm glad to have you for a friend."

She offered him a tight-lipped smile. "Thanks."

She left the apartment, unable to get home soon enough and to begin the long process of forgetting.

It was a glorious early summer morning. Sun streamed through the trees and a soft breeze stirred their tender new leaves. Clusters of rosebuds dangled on trellises, and lawns were green and lush.

Hadley pushed Nicky in his stroller. Walking briskly, she calculated they'd gone a good half mile. But the restless energy inside her remained.

Summer was a time of growth. So, it seemed fitting she'd come to the conclusion she had. Now that Drake was getting back in circulation, she needed to meet a nice man or two. She needed to go out herself. Drake had made her realize she was capable of feeling again. She just needed to direct her feelings toward the right man, a sensible man, a one-woman man, a man with a job that entailed no risks. The trouble was she didn't know anyone who was available, unless she counted that Certified Public Accountant that Aunt Margaret had mentioned. It seemed that the dentist had fallen into the clutches of someone named Lisette. Lately, Aunt Margaret had been dropping hints about the CPA.

She wheeled the stroller past Mr. Knickerbocker's, noticing that his scraped and dinged Buick was gone again. She turned up the brick sidewalk leading to her house and took Nicky inside, leaving the stroller on the porch.

She put on a kettle of water for tea and punched in Aunt Margaret's number, figuring she might as well take the plunge.

"Dear, I'll be there as soon as the cosmetics lady leaves. I'm ordering a new lipstick shade—'Red Alert.' "

Twenty minutes later, Aunt Margaret's convertible appeared in the driveway. Her hair was freshly done in a short, youthful style.

She came through the front door like a warm breeze, planting a Red Alert smudge on Nicky's cheek. Hadley got a hug.

"Tea sounds lovely, especially with your macaroons," she said, smelling of a dizzying clash of perfume samples.

"Tell me what you've been up to, Aunt Margaret." She poured two cups of mint tea at the kitchen table.

"Oh, that would take too long. I'm much more interested in what you've been doing. I drove by not long ago and saw Drake Matthieson's Jeep."

"We were discussing Callie," she said matter-of-factly.

The older woman nibbled delicately at the edge of a macaroon, but said nothing. However, Hadley knew that she was thinking plenty.

"Aunt Margaret, I was wondering about that man at the bank that you were telling me about—the CPA. Maybe it wouldn't be such a bad idea for you to introduce us."

Her eyes lit up and she put her macaroon down. "Do you really mean that?"

She nodded.

"I'd love to introduce you. He's just the nicest thing—and handsome, too."

Hadley toyed with the rim of her cup. "It has been three years now, and . . . I've decided it's time to move forward."

The older woman reached out and patted her hand. "I'm

glad you feel that way. I've been waiting for the day that you would say that." She settled back into her chair. "Now, about Noland: He's got 'family man' written all over him. The only problem is that the right woman hasn't come along yet." She followed with a wink that was pure matchmaker.

"Slow down, Aunt Margaret. I didn't say anything about marrying him. I might not even like him."

"Oh, but you will," she insisted. "He opens doors for the elderly. He stands up when a lady enters the room. I'd adopt him, but I'm sure he's already got a mother."

Nervously, Hadley stirred her tea. He certainly sounded safe enough. She hoped for her sake that he was all that and more— enough to make her stop thinking about Drake.

"And he already likes you. I can tell," she said.

Hadley squinted at her. "How could he like me? We've never met."

"I've told him all about you."

"You didn't," she said with mild dismay.

"I did. Come with me to the bank on Monday," she urged. "I need to get a little cash."

She had to admit that he was everything Aunt Margaret said. He was courteous and polite, and he stood when they approached his desk. With thick, closely cropped dark blond hair and blue eyes, he was good-looking in a subtle, buttoned-down way. He was an inch or two under six feet and had a runner's build. Unlike Drake, he wasn't apt to make a woman stop what she was doing when he entered a room. Rather, he was a man of quieter attributes.

He surprised her by calling just a day later. One of the bank's clients was opening a new Greek restaurant. Would she like to try it with him?

After she hung up, she was as flustered as a schoolgirl, except that she was no teenager. She was twenty-seven years old and starting over. It had been six years since she'd had a date, discounting, of course, the "date" with Drake. She wasn't sure she knew the rules anymore.

There had been a safe predictability in the life she'd been leading. She'd forged her grief into a manageable numbness, shutting down that part of her heart that a woman reserves for a man. Only with Nicky was her love free, boundless and without reservation. Now, she was entering a new phase, but not without trepidation.

She called Aunt Margaret to take her up on her standing offer to baby-sit. But this time, the request was followed by an uncharacteristic beat of silence.

"Oh, dear, it's the weekend of my tole painting association's annual convention in Denver. I have hotel reservations."

Hadley tried Kelly across the street, but she had a new part-time job at the Burger Blitz. She referred Hadley to a friend named Amanda. But as it turned out, Amanda already had a babysitting job for that night.

Hadley nervously strummed the kitchen counter. Just maybe this wasn't meant to be. After all, she didn't like the idea of leaving Nicky with a stranger. He was going through a clingy stage and she wanted to leave him with someone he knew and liked. Unfortunately, her list of options was exhausted—except for one person.

She got up and paced around the kitchen. This time, he owed her. Yet she didn't want to ask. Wasn't the point of going out with Noland to get Drake *out* of her life?

She'd postpone the date. What choice did she have? Surely, Noland would understand.

Before she could get to the phone, the doorbell rang. She rushed through the living room and peeked through the lace curtain on the front door. Her heart stumbled.

Drake stood on the porch. On his face was the suggestion of a smile. "I've been shopping. Could I bother you just a few minutes for an opinion?"

The late afternoon sun brought out a few glints of silver in his hair. On his cheeks, was a day's growth of beard. For a moment, all she could do was look at him. He was a picture postcard unto himself. Why did he keep doing this to her—showing up and looking so distractedly masculine?

"What sort of opinion?" she finally managed to ask.

He turned toward the Jeep. It was stuffed with bags of unidentifiable objects. "I bought some things for my apartment. I want to know what you think."

After checking to make sure Nicky was still napping, she walked with Drake to the car. He opened the door and grabbed a large bag containing three plump pillows covered in a multi-colored fabric of a geometric pattern that resembled Native American weavings. "The saleslady helped," he said.

"They're very nice."

He looked pleased. He tossed the pillows back in the bag and grabbed a rolled rug. He unfurled it on the sidewalk. It resembled a Navaho design and was woven in muted dark colors. "What do you think of this?" he asked.

"I like it. It has style, but is masculine at the same time. It should go well with your other things, but you won't really know until you take them home and put them all together."

He nodded. "Just a taste check. I'm a guy who has trouble picking out a tie."

"You did just fine, Drake."

"Why don't you come over Saturday and take a look? This is not exactly a guy thing, you know. I don't want to send women heading for the exits."

"I assure you that's not going to happen. Besides, I'm busy Saturday. I have a date."

His expression froze. "What?"

"I have a dinner date with a man Aunt Margaret introduced me to."

He leaned against the side of the Jeep and folded his arms across his chest. "Do I know him?" His voice was uncharacteristically soft.

"I don't think so. He works at the bank."

He bit the inside of his cheek and studied her a moment. "He'd better be a damned nice guy."

The fervor in his tone surprised her. "You sound like somebody watching out for his kid sister."

He shoved his hands in his pockets. "I'm a guy watching out for a special friend."

She stared at him. His eyes were narrowed with a rare hint of emotion, one she couldn't define. "Don't worry. Aunt Margaret thinks he's Mr. Perfect."

"Sometimes you've got to watch guys like that." His tone was heavy with cop cynicism.

Hadley placed her hands on her hips in a show of mild annoyance. "Drake, are you thinking like a friend or a policeman?"

"Both."

"He's the president of the Mountain Spring Civic Club, for heaven's sake. Aunt Margaret said they just raised a record amount of money for a children's hospital."

He rubbed his hand over the stubble on his jaw.

"If I didn't know better, I'd say you were acting as if you were jealous," she said.

His gaze turned as sharp as an icicle. "You have my complete support, Hadley. It's just that you're special. You're one of our own. I want the best for you."

A lull of silence passed between them. "That's very sweet of you," she said. Her voice was strained.

"And just to prove I'm not jealous and that you have my total support, I'll baby-sit."

Her heart thumped. "Oh, no, that's not necessary. I . . ."

"Is your aunt going to sit with him?"

"She can't—at least the way things are scheduled now, but I'm trying to . . ."

"Let's make it simple, Hadley," he interjected. "I'll do it. I like Nicky and he likes me. I'm somewhat experienced—at least with Nicky—and I come with good references, if the Denver Police Department counts for anything. I know CPR, the Heimlich maneuver and advanced first aid."

"But what about your social life? Don't you have plans?"

He shrugged. "After being out of the saddle for a year or so, I suppose I could wait another week."

Fresh out of logical rebuttals, Hadley relented. She knew Nicky would be happier with Drake than anyone.

"Case closed?" he asked.

She responded with a freighted sigh. "I guess. Noland is coming to pick me up Saturday at seven. I'll have everything ready for you."

Drake decided that appearing in full uniform for a baby-sitting gig might be a bit much. Instead, he wore jeans, commando boots and a police t-shirt, one that had shrunken somewhat and showed his biceps off to good advantage. That would make this Noland guy think twice about moving in on Hadley too fast. After all, there were a lot of strange characters out there, many of them masquerading as normal. One had to be careful these days. She should know that.

Taking the Mountain Spring exit, he dismissed once again the notion that he could be jealous. What could have made her say such a thing? Well, he'd shown her. Jealous guys don't offer to baby-sit so their female friends can go out on dates.

A few minutes later, he pulled up next to the curb in front of Hadley's house, giving wide berth to Mr. Knickerbocker's Buick, which was zigzagging out of the driveway. He parked the Jeep a safe distance away and grabbed a new police magazine from the front seat. He'd catch up on his reading while Nicky was asleep. He checked his watch. It was six-thirty.

He got out, noticing that Hadley's house looked even more homey than usual. There was some kind of wreath on the door with sprigs of flowers stuck in it and there were window boxes on the two front sills. Ivy trailed out of them along with some plants he couldn't name. His mind flashed back to the flowers his mother used to plant and to the foster home where only weeds seemed to grow.

He straightened his shoulders and rang the doorbell. He heard her footsteps. They made a brisk, rhythmic sound on the oak floor. Until he'd met Hadley, he'd never given much thought to anything as trite as a woman's footsteps. Somehow, he liked the sound of hers.

The lace curtain lifted, then dropped, and the deadbolt turned.

"Hi, Drake. Come in."

She sounded a bit too cheerful to suit him.

When Nicky came running toward him with his little gap-toothed smile, something inside him went soft. What was happening to him?

"How's my top man in Mountain Spring?" he asked.

"He's fine," Hadley answered. "He's already had his supper. All you have to do is put him to bed around eight-thirty."

She was dressed in black pants with a short, matching jacket. Under the jacket was some sort of little white knit top that dipped a few inches under the little well in her throat. She looked tailored, but very, very sexy. Damn it.

"Don't worry," he said, trying to keep his eyes off the creamy skin between her lapels, "Nick and I can hold things together."

"There's milk and juice in the refrigerator, and fresh sugar cookies in the cookie jar. There's also roast beef if you're in the mood for a sandwich."

He barely heard her. He was looking at her beautiful rose-colored mouth and thinking thoughts he shouldn't have.

"If you'll watch Nicky, I'll finish getting ready," she said, clicking off to the bedroom in black pumps.

Drake put the boy down and gave him a conspiratorial wink. "She's the one who needs watching, right?"

Nicky smiled innocently. Drake ruffled the toddler's hair. He seemed to have grown a couple of inches since he'd first seen him strapped every which way in that medieval fortress of a child carrier. In the blink of an eye, he'd be a teenager. In another blink, he'd be gone. As Drake grew older, he was amazed and somewhat dismayed at how fast time could slip away.

They played a quick game, tossing colored plastic rings over a peg. Then Drake heard a car door slam. His spine stiffened and he stepped to the window. Through the louvers of the shutters he saw a man with blondish-brown hair and a slim build. The guy was wearing a suit that, even from a distance, appeared to be pressed to perfection.

Drake sized him up with the acuity of a veteran crime fighter, and he had to concede: The man had law-abiding citizen written all over him. Drake looked at his atomic watch. He was prompt, too. It was seven o'clock straight up. The ring of the doorbell brought a hard knot to his gut. He stretched up to his full height and opened the door.

The man looked at Drake in mild surprise. "I'm Noland Fletcher. I've come for Hadley."

Drake took a perverse satisfaction in noting that this Fletcher character was about three inches shorter than he was. "I'm

Drake Matthieson—Police Lt. Drake Matthieson," he couldn't resist adding. "I'm a friend of Hadley's. Please come in."

Hadley rushed in, her golden hair sleekly brushed. "Hi, Noland." There was a bothersome lilt to her voice. "Have you met Drake? He's baby-sitting for me tonight."

"We've met."

"And, of course, you remember Nicky. He was with me at the bank."

"Hi, little fellow."

Nicky retreated shyly behind Hadley's leg. She turned, knelt and gave him a kiss on the forehead. "Be good for Drake. Mommy will be home in a few hours."

Saying he was pleased to have met Drake and again holding out his hand, Noland demonstrated his perfect manners before leaving in his perfect suit. Drake couldn't remember the last time he'd worn one himself.

As soon as the front door closed, Drake jumped to the window, tipped a louver and mentally jotted down Noland's license plate number. He watched him open the door for Hadley, then back out in his sensible gray sedan.

Drake popped the louver back into place and took a deep breath. The woman had crossed a milestone in her life. He should be happy for her. But to his horror, he wasn't all that happy for himself.

Hadley pretended to look interested as Noland talked about the new accounting software. All evening, he'd been sweetly attentive, opening doors, pulling out chairs and making sure the wine suited her. Yet, if the conversation so far counted for anything, they didn't seem to have much in common.

Drake seldom talked about his work, despite undoubtedly having a spellbinding repertoire of tales. For all his faults, which seemed to decrease in number as the evening went on, Drake did know how to make a woman laugh.

Hadley toyed with the moussaka on her plate. She could have sworn she saw one of the louvers on the shutters snap open as they left. Had Drake been watching them?

She did learn that Noland enjoyed children and had spent days looking for just the right toy for his nephew's fourth birthday. But along with his admirable traits, Noland appeared to have some strange ones. He dusted off his chair before he sat in it. And he didn't want any of the foods on his plate to touch. He'd told the waiter so.

Drake didn't mind a little dirt. In fact, sometimes the dirtier he got, the more irresistible he looked, like the time he'd come in from hanging the gutter with a smudge on his cheek and a tear in his shirt.

Drake ate heartily and went back for seconds. Noland ate fussily. He'd removed all the cucumber slices from his salad and segregated them on the rim of his plate as if he were weeding a garden.

"What do you think, Hadley?" Noland asked, jolting her from her comparative musings.

Her cheeks turned warm. She looked at him uncomprehendingly.

"Do you think banks could be more customer-friendly?"

"Oh, I think they're doing a pretty good job," she groped. "Of course, there's always room for improvement."

On the way home, it didn't get much better. She found herself missing Drake's wit and his grudging smiles. The realization of it horrified her.

Noland pulled up in the driveway and carefully set the emergency brake. Hadley noticed that the porch light had been turned on.

"I've enjoyed the evening, Hadley," he said. "Maybe we can do it again sometime."

"Maybe we can," she said politely. But she knew what "maybe" meant. It meant that he wasn't committing himself. It probably meant that he, like she, knew this wasn't really working.

He walked her to the porch and turned toward her. He took her wrists in his hands. "Good night."

"Good night, Noland. It was a lovely dinner."

He leaned forward and kissed her lightly on her cheekbone. Her heart thumped in surprise. He released her hands and walked away.

For a moment, she stood on the porch and touched her fingers to the spot where he'd kissed her. It was a very sweet gesture, really. Maybe she'd judged things too hastily.

The front door was unlocked. She stepped inside to find Drake sitting on the sofa with one long leg crossed over the other. He put down the police magazine he was reading and got up.

"You should always keep the door deadbolted," she said.

A corner of his mouth sneaked upward as he looked at her with a gaze as clear as a mountain stream. She'd missed him more than she'd thought.

"I thought I'd save you the trouble of opening it."

"How's Nicky?"

"Out like a light and has been since eight-thirty."

"He didn't give you any trouble?"

"Nope. I wore him out playing baseball. By the way, sorry about the glass over the picture. I'll get another piece for it."

Hadley glanced at a narrow table against the wall where she kept an assortment of family photographs. Across the picture of her grandmother as a girl was a diagonal crack.

"Nicky's pitching arm is still a little underdeveloped," he said.

Hadley examined the picture. Satisfied the print itself wasn't damaged, she put it down.

"How was the date?"

Tonight, he looked especially handsome for no particular reason other than she was comparing him to Noland.

"I had a lovely time," she said, applying a little torque to the truth. Honesty was not the best policy here.

He gave her a little tight-lipped smile. "I'm glad."

An awkward silence followed. Hadley took a few steps across the room. Everything was neat and in its place. The toys had been put away. Only a few magazines, one with a screaming headline on high-speed chases, were scattered about. She remembered the debris left in the wake of Drake's first baby-sitting stint and she marveled at the contrast.

"Looks like you're getting the hang of things," she said.

"Yeah, well . . . Things get easier with practice."

She tiptoed into the bedroom to look at Nicky. Drake followed her. Through the combination of a nightlight and Mr. Knickerbocker's gaslight shining through the window, she could see him sleeping soundly. He even had his pajamas on and was properly tucked in. Drake was near enough that she could feel his body heat. Suddenly, standing in the dark with him and watching a child sleep seemed to be more intimacy than she could handle. She turned and walked out of the room.

"I should be going," Drake said as they reached the living room.

Hadley was relieved. At the same time, she wanted him to stay. "It was very nice of you to baby-sit. Thank you."

"Anytime," he said with a shrug. "When's the next date with Norris?"

"Noland," Hadley corrected.

His chin crinkled. "Sorry. When is it?"

Hadley scrambled for just the right words. "We haven't decided. But don't worry. There's always Aunt Margaret—

almost always."

He nodded stiffly. He grabbed his police magazine, tucked it under his arm like a schoolboy and walked to the door. He stopped, then after a second or two, turned back toward her. "I'm painting my living room green. Did I tell you?" He touched a sage-colored wall. "It's a lot like this."

Hadley was mildly surprised. It wasn't what she'd suggested. "I'm glad you like it."

"There's something about it. Anyway, thanks again for helping with my apartment. Good night, Hadley."

For a long time after he left, she sat on the sofa where he had sat. There they'd been, going through the motions of friendship and the casual and sometimes meaningless banter that conversation between friends often entails. All the while, her heart was screaming something else.

Her heart was telling her that her plan had backfired wretchedly. She'd gone out with someone safe and predictable, a man who had the right attributes for the secure and orderly life she wanted for herself and Nicky. She wanted someone who had a ninety-nine percent chance of returning home to his family every night.

But he wasn't Drake. And with that, she came to a deeper and yet more frightening realization: No one else ever could be.

CHAPTER TWELVE

The division headquarters out of which Drake worked was relatively quiet on Sundays. The radio exchanges with officers in the field were sporadic. The coffee pot was slow to empty. It was a perfect day to come in and do a little investigating.

In the Jeep, on the way here, he'd felt a little foolish, but not foolish enough to stay home and mind his own business. He was compelled to do this for reasons he didn't want to think about.

He went to a cluster of computers in a glassed-in area reserved for officers' use. He sat down and punched in a password. Within a few seconds, he had access to every license plate number in the state of Colorado.

He took from his shirt pocket a slip of the hot pink note paper that Hadley kept by her phone and entered the license number he'd jotted down. On the screen appeared basic data on the owner of the car.

For whatever it was worth, the car was properly registered to one Noland Fletcher, sex male, age 31, address in Mountain Springs' second most exclusive area. Using a key number gleaned from the registration, Drake went on to do a criminal background check.

Noland Norquist Fletcher had never even had a speeding ticket. What was more, he was an organ donor volunteer and had paid the extra two bucks over the price of his driver's license to go into a special fund for the blind.

Drake strummed his fingers on the keyboard. He was safe, all right. Clean as a whistle. Good enough for Hadley.

The realization caused something to sour within him. She deserved the best. But he couldn't know everything about this bean counter. What if he was doing something right now for which he hadn't been caught? Nope, fat chance of that. The guy was so honest that he probably wouldn't even pick up a dime lying on a sidewalk.

He folded his arms across his chest and leaned back in his chair. Mr. Perfect had even given her a goodnight kiss on the cheek. He knew because he'd been peeping through the tiniest crack in the shutters. It had made him ashamed of himself for looking. Worse, it had made him jealous.

He'd wanted to be the one to feel her satin skin against his lips and to smell the flowery fragrance in her hair. Hell's bells. Was a visit to the cop shrink in order? He couldn't remember ever feeling this way before about anyone.

She was everything he didn't need. He was everything she didn't want. There was only one thing to do: He had to forget about waiting until he got his apartment fixed up. He needed to get back in circulation immediately. That would be the best thing for him, and the best thing for Hadley. He'd still be there if she needed him but he hoped that she never would.

For the next few evenings, after Nicky had been put to bed, Hadley went back to her computer to finish up the police car designs. Her objective was to finish ahead of schedule, to cut ties to Drake as soon as possible.

There were three designs—one traditional; one innovative, spelling out "police" in a bold, leaning backhand along the side of the car, and a combination of the two. The bold one was her favorite. It incorporated the city seal. She'd done that one with Drake in mind. After a rough start in which the ideas just wouldn't flow, she'd managed to outdo herself on all of them. She didn't want to have to go back to the drawing board, to have to prolong the project.

She printed out five sets of designs, one for each committee member and put them in presentation folders. When she finished, it was past two-thirty in the morning. But she was finished—four days ahead of schedule.

Hadley went to bed, but she couldn't sleep. She felt an odd emptiness after finishing the project, not just for herself but for Nicky.

Nicky had dragged out his plastic ball and bat several times and mimicked what was probably Drake's expert swing. She'd taken him outside and played ball with him herself to show him subtly he didn't need Drake to have a good time. But she was so clumsy that half the balls ended up on the ground before they reached the plate—the "plate" being a bath towel tossed over the grass.

Baseball aside, Drake had held some sort of magic for Nicky, even from the beginning. He'd shied away from Noland. There she went, comparing them again.

The next morning, when it was barely eight o'clock, she called the commander and told him that the proposals were ready. She'd drive them up or overnight them. To her consternation, he said he'd send Drake after them. They'd agreed on two o'clock on Saturday afternoon. That way, he'd be able to look over them during the weekend.

It occurred to her suddenly and with considerable trepidation that the commander might be an undercover matchmaker. Hadn't Drake once mentioned that his old partner had told him that he ought to settle down?

Drake surprised her by showing up two hours early. She was

planting begonias in the flowerbeds in the front yard. The knees of her denim overalls were muddy and her forehead was gritty from wiping strands of hair out of her eyes with the back of a dirty gardening glove. All things considered, it shouldn't have mattered that she was a mess, but it did.

She stood as he got out of the Jeep and strolled toward her. He carried a pizza box. Nicky dropped the empty plastic nursery pots he'd been playing with and ran toward him in his clumsy toddler's gait. Drake lifted him with his free arm and planted him back on the ground with a smile on his face.

Uneasily, Hadley glanced at Nicky's socks to make sure they hadn't been charmed off. Then she took off her gloves and tossed them toward the porch. She missed.

"Good shot." The sun danced over Drake's hair.

Hadley shot him a look of mild annoyance and looked at her watch. She had to wipe off a smudge of dirt to read it. "You're right on time—Eastern Standard Time."

"Yeah, well, sorry . . . But I brought lunch, loaded with everything they had. They remembered me from my rookie days in Mountain Spring and started piling it on. I knew you liked artichoke parts and . . ."

"Artichoke hearts," she corrected with amusement.

He gave her a tight-lipped smile that left her resistance wavering.

"Come on," he urged, "before Nicky and I eat it all ourselves."

They ate outside on a small brick patio that Hadley had laid herself with used bricks and sand. They sat in director's chairs around a round metal table decorated with a few of Nicky's crayon scribblings. Nibbling happily on a small piece of pizza, the boy swung his red-sneakered feet back and forth like scissors. He watched Drake with bald admiration.

Hadley wiped a smudge of sauce off the boy's nose in order to distract him. She sneaked a quick glance at Drake. He was gently picking a ladybug off the sleeve of his denim shirt. He placed it on the palm of his hand and held it out for Nicky to see. Then he let it fly away.

For a man whose own childhood had been one trauma after another, he was amazingly adept at making a child smile.

"I bought a box of them," she said of the ladybugs. "They help keep the bad bugs off the plants."

Her words sounded trite and pedestrian in contrast to the thoughts racing through her head.

He touched the begonia in the small clay pot in the center of the table. Then he surprised her by taking her hand in his and examining her thumb.

"That figures," he said.

"What do you mean?"

"It seems to have a slight greenish cast. The proverbial green thumb."

She gently pulled her hand away, but the heat of his touch remained.

"How's the apartment coming?" she asked, attempting to keep the conversation from getting too intimate.

"Still working on it."

"Do you have a date set for the grand opening?"

"No, but the new receptionist at the station has offered to help speed things up. She claims to be handy with a roller and a brush. In addition, she walks with a provocative little wiggle."

Hadley managed a smile, but her insides reacted like she was on a high-speed elevator headed forty floors down.

A brief, but awkward, silence fell between them.

"And Noland," he said, tentatively, breaking the lull. "Are you seeing him tonight?"

She thought quickly. "Not tonight." That implied there would be another night, which she was not sure there would be. He studied her, obviously hoping she'd say more. She didn't.

"Do you like him?" he ventured.

"You certainly are nosy."

"Well, do you?" His eyes shone with curiosity.

"Of course, I do. He couldn't be nicer."

His mouth twisted slightly. "I don't doubt that. He reminded me of Wesley Gerhardt in the first grade. He came to school already knowing how to read and he was the teacher's pet. I hated him."

Mildly perturbed, Hadley frowned at him. "Your receptionist sounds like a cross between Betty Boop and Mae West."

Drake laughed. His was a rich, melodious laugh that sent lines fanning out from the corners of his eyes.

Hadley's irritation grew. "What's so funny?"

"You've got Adrian all wrong. She's top-notch professional. She can even type and learned all our names in short order. She can spell them, too, even Niebeisczcanski's. She speaks passable Spanish, too. As for her wiggle, it just happens to be a bonus."

"It's reassuring to know I'm getting a bonus for my tax dollars."

He grinned crookedly. Suddenly, his cell phone chirped. He took it from his belt and punched the talk button. "Matthieson."

She watched as his smile faded. Her emotions shifted into an anxiety mode.

"When?" he asked.

Hadley thought she actually saw his face pale.

"I'll be there as soon as I can." He switched off the phone and looked at her. "I have to go. A surveillance team has picked up something."

"I thought you were off today."

"It doesn't matter. They know I want to be around for this one." He rose quickly. "Sit tight. I should be back this evening."

"Be careful."

That was all she could say before he sprinted through the back gate.

Her heartbeat strummed in her ears. The birds, which had seemed to be singing so merrily, appeared to fall silent. Nicky started to fuss.

She looked at the half-eaten piece of pizza on Drake's plate. She knew what life with a policeman was like. It was living in one-day increments. Another day on the job. Another evening home safe. She thought she'd been conditioned, yet the intensity of feeling she'd had when Drake hurried away had left her stunned. She sat quietly for a moment, wondering and worrying. Not even a day off was sacred for this consummate cop. Her imagination raced out of control until out of sheer willpower, she managed to rein it in.

She kept busy. She finished planting the begonias in neat rows that followed the curves of the flowerbeds. Behind them, she planted a row of caladiums with pale green and white-veined leaves. When that was done, she strapped Nicky into the mini-van and took him to a toy store. She took care not to spoil him, preferring instead to make playthings out of old kitchen utensils and cardboard boxes. But today, she was given another reminder that life is a tenuous proposition. It didn't hurt to splurge just once in a while.

They left the toy store with a silly green dinosaur that growled when squeezed, then stopped for ice cream. Nicky got vanilla in a tiny child's cone; she got pineapple ice in a cup.

Afterwards, they went to a nearby park where Nicky took delight in riding a yellow hippopotamus set on a thick spring. Hadley sat on a bench and watched him, trying in vain not to think of Drake.

When they got home, it was just five o'clock. It had seemed much later. The light on the answering machine signaled no messages.

Time dragged. Her worry intensified. He'd been gone four hours. Despite having the new dinosaur, Nicky hauled out the little plastic ball and bat again. She pitched the ball in the back yard. He managed to hit it twice, his face lighting up like a lightning bug.

Another half hour passed. Her heart beat a hard rhythm in her chest. She cooked a light supper of scrambled eggs, ham and toast. She watched over Nicky's meal, leaving her own half untouched.

The clock inched slowly toward eight o'clock. Her nerves jumped at every bump and thump that suggested the opening or closing of a car door. At one point, she'd rushed to the front door, her blood racing with hope, only to find that it was Mr. Knickerbocker returning home from the senior citizens' dance. She turned away from the shutters with a twist of disappointment.

She gave Nicky a bath, trying to feign reasonably good cheer. Children, no matter how young, sensed things. She put on his pajamas and put him to bed. She read him *Goldilocks and the Three Bears*. It was their normal routine, yet tonight was different. There was stillness in the air. She could feel its cold weight settling over her.

As the night wore on, she grew more and more uneasy. She sat on the sofa with a magazine on her lap, but she couldn't seem to get past the first paragraph of an article on the terrible two's. So far, nothing about Nicky had been terrible.

She put it down and looked at her watch again. She got up and began to pace. Could it only be eight-forty? Minutes seemed to be turning into hours.

How could a raid, if that was what it was, take seven hours? She thought they just burst in with guns and ramrods and it was over. Unless . . .

Half paralyzed with worry, she made a call to Drake's division. A dispatcher, sounding somewhat evasive, asked her to call back in an hour.

A flood of shallowly buried memories engulfed her: the crosses on the lapels of the police chaplain; the harsh feel of a flag folded into a triangle. She thought of Drake, a man with seemingly no fears except a fear of loving.

And it was then that she realized she loved him.

The realization was raw and shattering. She took a gasping breath and sat down. She could avoid him all she wanted. She could go out with endless made-for-marriage Nolands. She could move to Bora Bora. But she wouldn't be able to get him out of her heart.

She loved Drake because of his innate goodness, for qualities that would be there long after his hair turned silver and his gait slowed. He was tough enough to fight for what was right, to put the problems of others before his own. He was gentle enough to reach a teenager and to coax a smile out of a child.

But he didn't love her, and somehow that was easier to accept than the fact she loved him. She had everything to lose—again.

Suddenly, she heard the snap of a car door outside. Her heart scrambling to her throat, she leaped to the door. The porch light had been burning for hours. She threw back the lace curtain to find Drake coming up the sidewalk. Her spirits went into a heady upward spiral.

She said a barely-suppressed prayer of thanks and opened the door. She wanted to run into his arms, but she held back. Instead, she just looked at him, taking in his very essence.

He grinned crookedly. "I'm not that big of a mess, am I?"

He stepped inside. It was then that she noticed the bandage barely visible across the neckline of his denim shirt. And as he stood near the bright light of a nearby lamp, she could see a nasty scrape on his jaw.

"Oh, Drake . . ."

He stepped forward, and the next thing she knew, she was in his arms. He pulled her body firmly against his and her blood pulsed wildly at the feel of his hard body along the length of her. He kissed the delicate area where her shoulder met her neck. He kissed her earlobe. He kissed her cheekbone. His lips lingered at her temple until she almost begged him to kiss her mouth.

Achingly slow, he got there. His lips came down hungrily on hers, their heat reaching her soul. He pulled back and looked at her, his eyes murky with desire. Then, he kissed her again, this time with lightness and constraint.

Stunned, all she could do for a moment was stare into his glistening gray eyes. She placed her fingers on his shoulder. She could feel the stiff binding underneath.

"What happened?" It seemed a moot question to ask him if he was all right. There couldn't be anything seriously wrong with a man who kissed like that.

"Just a sprain," he said. "I went up against a concrete floor."

Hadley felt an ache as if it had been her own shoulder. "I was worried about you."

"Yeah, well I was worried about me, too, for a few seconds. A guy jumped down on top of me from an attic opening. He wasn't armed, but he was trying to be—with my gun."

She went cold inside. He'd won this time, just like all the others, but what about the next? Could the odds continue to run in his favor? Suddenly looking very tired, he pulled her close again and just held her, saying nothing. His fingers slipped underneath her loose, white cotton shirt and he made lazy, explorative circles with his fingertips over the sensitive skin along her spine.

She melted against him, laying her cheek against the broad expanse of his chest. Her heart raced. His thundered back at her as she felt the muscular contours of his shoulder.

He framed her face in his hands and kissed her once again, this time with an undercurrent of desperation. Then suddenly, they both pulled away from each other as if they'd reached the same conclusion at the same time.

He gazed at her, his eyes dulled with need, his breath ragged. "You know we can't keep doing this, don't you? We could end up going someplace we shouldn't be going."

She nodded, her throat thick with emotion. "We shouldn't be here together at all," she said, stepping back.

He dropped his hands from her shoulders. "What just happened . . . Maybe we could just chalk it up to the stress of the evening."

"Worry can make people irrational." Her explanation seemed just as hollow as his.

He placed a hand on his forehead and looked down as if he needed a moment to get his bearings. "Can you get me the drawings?"

Suddenly, his tone was so coolly professional that she was startled by the contrast.

"The commander is expecting them."

She took him into her office where the neatly labeled folders still lay on her desk. She handed him the one on top. Her head was still spinning, not just from his kisses but how her body had played back to him like music in counterpoint.

He opened the folder, looked over the designs, and then pointed at one. "This is it."

The bold, contemporary design was the one Hadley predicted he'd pick. "It's my favorite, too."

"Now, it's up to the committee."

"When will they decide?" Even though they were talking business, her heart was speaking another language. She struggled not to let it show.

"Monday afternoon." He spoke as if he weren't struggling with anything at all.

"Let me know if you'd like to make any changes. I'd like for everybody to be happy." She handed him the other folders. He nodded. An awkward pause followed. Suddenly, they were looking at each other like a couple of adolescents after a fumbled first kiss.

"I'll be in touch," he said finally. His fingers grazed her shoulder lightly and then he was gone.

For a time afterward, Hadley stood by the door, unable to move. Her mind reeled. Her pulse strummed. They couldn't be "friends" anymore, not like this. Maybe he could walk away from his feelings, but she couldn't.

Tonight, her lines of defense had been breached. Now that the project was finished, now was the time to tell him that it was time for their "friendship" to end as well.

To pretend that they could just be friends was a charade that she couldn't endure any longer. To have him keep popping in and out of her life would only prolong the pain. In life, he had a nine-year head start on her. He'd set his course long ago, and it wasn't going to change. And she understood. They had different goals—permanence and stability for her; impermanence and risk for him. He didn't need a wife any more than she needed to be a widow again.

That alone should have been enough to stop her from loving him, but it wasn't.

Now, she had to do the only rational thing she could—to move forward—without him. All she had to do was to tell him.

A few days later, he called, saying he had good news. The committee had unanimously approved the logo design—*their* logo. He'd bring by some information about the company that would actually apply the design to the cars. They would be contacting her for the next stage of the project.

She hung up. All it had taken for her pulse to go wild again was the sound of his voice.

He came the following Saturday afternoon. She'd barely opened the door when Nicky slipped past her and locked his arms around one of his long, denim-clad legs.

"Hey, how's my point man?"

Nicky looked up at him, his face glowing with hero worship. Hadley's insides shriveled.

Drake's eyes met hers in an instant of silent communication, then their sparkle faded. He looked fit and handsome. His skin had taken on a rosy bronze color as the summer wore on. She could tell by the bulk under his shirt that his shoulder was still taped.

"How are you, Hadley?" The question sounded oddly formal.

"Fine. How's your shoulder?"

"Better, thanks."

Hadley took Nicky's hand and gently led him away from Drake. "Please come in."

Drake handed her a folder marked 'Design Committee.' "I thought maybe we could go for a walk. I've got something to tell you." His expression was serious.

Hadley's stomach tightened. "All right. It just so happens that I have something to say as well."

She laid the folder on a small table inside the door and put Nicky in a little red wagon parked next to the steps. Drake took the handle and began to pull.

They were a half block away before either of them said anything. She was thinking of how much they looked like a family, how their steps moved in the same rhythm, how this would be the last walk they ever took together. She would tell him when they got to the park.

He was the first to break the silence. "Hadley, I hope I haven't led you to expect more from me than what I can give."

She stopped under the shade of one of the large, old trees lining the street and turned toward him, her cheeks warming. "What makes you think that I'm expecting anything?"

A muscle flexed in his jaw. "I didn't mean to sound presumptuous."

"You would have to be to assume I'm just another hapless candidate for the Drake Matthieson Broken Hearts Club."

"Hadley, I was just trying to make sure we understood each other." His voice contained a rare hint of emotion.

"I understand perfectly," she said indignantly. "Unlike those legions of women who thought they could pierce your armor, I know you're out of reach. I know what it means to be held by you. I know what it means to be kissed by you. I know it means nothing."

He took her firmly by the shoulders. His chin crinkled stubbornly. A storm brewed in his eyes. "Don't say it didn't mean anything to me, because nothing could be further from the truth."

She took a step backward, freeing herself from his grasp. "I'm not a girl, Drake. I'm a woman who has experienced life. There's no need to pretend."

His eyes narrowed. "If you think I'd ever try to lead you astray, you're wrong. You have to believe me when I say that I care very much for you. But our friendship has gotten out of bounds. Maybe what has happened between us is nothing but chemistry. Whatever it is, I think it would be a good idea if we backed off—for good. Maybe we shouldn't see each other again."

She stared at him numbly. Those were her lines and he'd stolen them from her, along with her dignity.

She straightened her spine. "I was going to suggest the same thing."

His mouth twisted, almost as if he were in pain, but he said nothing.

She took the handle of the wagon from him. "Feel free to go, Drake."

He continued to stand there, his gaze dark and intense.

"Thanks for everything." She softened her tone, dispelling some of the tension that hung in the air. She could at least remember her manners. She was angry that he would suggest that her heart was the only one at risk, but she wasn't ungrateful for all he'd done for her and Nicky. And there had been so much.

"My pleasure," he said stiffly. He leaned over and kissed Nicky on the crown. "Well, little guy, I guess this is it. Take good care of your mom."

A lump formed in her throat. She lifted her hand in a wave, not trusting her voice enough to say good-bye.

"We both agree this is for the best," he said.

She nodded.

"Good-bye, Hadley."

Her anger turned to a stinging humiliation as he turned and walked away, free and seemingly unscathed.

"Dake!" Nicky called after him. "Daaake!"

But he didn't turn back.

Chapter Thirteen

The apartment wasn't finished. Heck, he'd hardly even started. The pillows and the rugs were still in their bags. The painting supplies sat in the corner, untouched. Somehow, Drake had lost his motivation.

He'd had to break up with women before, but it wasn't anything like saying good-bye to Hadley. The pain of that had sliced into his very core. He'd done the right thing. The trouble was that it didn't feel right.

He was watching a baseball game. He had put the television on "mute" during a razor commercial and hadn't bothered to turn on the sound again. His shoulder still ached some, reminding him that he wasn't getting any younger. He was using the sprain as just another excuse not to tackle the apartment, but the real reason was Hadley. It was hard to imagine being with another woman and that scared the hell out of him.

He got up and began to pace around the room. He realized what he'd done. With the paint and the pillows, he was bringing Hadley into his life in the only safe way he dared. With her, he'd felt at home in a way that had nothing to do with sage green walls.

Tomorrow, he'd take the rugs and pillows back. He was stuck with the custom-mixed paint. He might even get a different apartment, one with new furniture. Furniture that would symbolize a new start. In all likelihood, the walls would be white, and he'd leave them that way. The move wouldn't be hard. He didn't have much in the way of personal belongings.

He glanced back at the television. The players seemed to get younger every year. Most of them were even younger than Hadley. He didn't know what the score was, and at that moment, it didn't matter. What did matter was forgetting those gorgeous blue eyes and that tousled mop of golden hair.

His social comeback was *going to start* with Adrian, the receptionist with the wiggle and the come-hither voice. By the time he'd gotten around to asking her out, she'd already been snatched up by a paramedic. At least his encounter with Brie had shown that he still had it.

He'd called Jodi Mason, who had been philosophically opposed to marriage when they'd last dated. As it turned out, she'd gone out and gotten herself hitched.

But then there was a female firefighter at Fire Station 27 who had been very friendly. They'd met at the frozen food section at the grocery store where she'd bought one of those healthy fish dinners with vegetables. He'd opted for something more substantial—meatloaf and mashed potatoes. With an inflection in her voice that sounded more like a hint than a casual inquiry, she asked if he was coming to the Fire Department's annual charity carnival. There had been enough heat in her tone to start a grass fire.

Drake thought about her for a moment. She was tall, with thick, straight, dark hair that just grazed her shoulders. Her smile was bright, her body firm and fit. She wasn't Hadley, but who was? He had to start somewhere.

He walked into his bedroom and picked up the phone.

Routine was Hadley's answer to getting her life back in order. As the weeks went by, she spent most of her days at the computer, working on design projects. In the afternoons, she took Nicky for wagon rides. She cooked and she cleaned. On weekends, she visited Aunt Margaret, who was forming a wine-tasting club, when she wasn't busy trying to get the attention of a Mr. Kirtzmer. Hadley went on a nature walk, to a gardening show, and to a butterfly preserve. Anything that would be distracting. Next weekend, it would be the Firefighters' Carnival. She managed to fill her days, but the nights were long and empty and haunted by questions.

How could Drake have kissed her the way he had if she meant nothing to him? How could he seem so at ease with Nicky on his shoulders? She understood that his work would always be the love of his life. And she would spend the rest of her life in fear for him. It was too late to change that.

Worse, she'd come to realize in the days afterwards that she not only loved him, but that she didn't want to live her life without him—regardless of the risks. That hurt most of all.

The Firefighters' Carnival was held in a vacant field where the town of Mountain Spring touched Denver's outermost city limit. At the entrance was a red fire engine so big and shiny that Hadley could see Nicky's reflection in it as they went by. Children climbed in, out and over the truck like ants, trying on firefighter's hats and taking turns "driving." Hadley paused to let Nicky watch a hefty firefighter transform a latex glove into a water balloon.

Green and white-striped tents rippled against a clear blue sky. The sun glinted off whirling rides. Recorded calliope music floated through the air. The soothing warmth of the early fall sunshine was a balm to her bruised heart.

Nicky almost climbed out of his stroller when he saw the merry-go-round with its prancing wooden steeds. Hadley handed an attendant a dollar and perched Nicky on a white horse with a red saddle. She held him tightly as the ride circled slowly to the tune of "The Blue Danube Waltz."

He rode in a kiddie car and in an airplane suspended from chains. With seemingly unlimited energy, Nicky insisted on pushing his own stroller. It was Hadley who was getting tired.

They stopped for ice cream, joining a waiting line of a half dozen people. Hadley had just finished reading a large menu posted on the front of the stand, when she turned back to Nicky. The stroller was there, but the spot where he had stood was empty.

She whirled around, looking in all directions. "Nicky?"

There was no response.

Her heart crashed against her ribs. She turned to an elderly couple in front of her. "Did you just see a little blond boy, two years old?"

The old man turned and peered at her through thick lenses. "Sure didn't, young lady."

Hadley, now frantic, left the stroller and tore away from the line. Scanning the crowd, she saw children of all ages, but not Nicky.

She knew from experience that his little legs could cover a lot of ground in a few seconds. He could be halfway out of the carnival by now. What if . . . She broke out in a cold sweat as she pushed desperately through the crowd.

"Looking for someone?" The voice was male and very familiar.

Hadley swung around to find Drake. He was holding Nicky. Weak with relief, she ran toward him and gathered the boy into her arms. For a moment, all she could do was hold his soft warmth against her.

"He saw me and just took off running," Drake said.

Hadley was so caught up in the moment that the rest of the world dissolved around her. When she looked up, she noticed the woman beside Drake.

She was tall, almost as tall as he was, with almond-shaped

green eyes and beautiful cheekbones. One hand was tucked possessively under his elbow.

"Hadley, I'd like for you to meet Melissa Giardelli. She's a firefighter."

Hadley summoned all the grace and poise she had, but it didn't seem quite enough. Her hand trembled slightly when she extended it. "I'm very pleased to meet you."

Melissa gripped hers firmly. "My pleasure as well."

Hadley tightened her hold on the toddler. "Nicky gave me quite a scare."

"I'm sorry," Drake said. "He surprised me, too. He just shot out of the blue."

"No harm done," Hadley replied. An awkward pause followed. "Well, we'd better get going."

A muscle twitched in Drake's jaw. "Good-bye, Hadley."

"So long." She struggled to maintain a casual tone.

He reached out and touched Nicky's head, then led Melissa away, her hand still tucked under his elbow.

Nicky lost hardly a second in protesting Drake's departure. He was little more than a step away when the boy let out a howl that caused passers-by to turn their heads. Hadley tightened her grip to keep him from wriggling out of her arms.

The noise prompted Melissa to turn back with a sympathetic smile. But Drake kept walking straight ahead.

Hadley did her best to quiet Nicky by stroking his hair. She wished she could tell him that Drake would be back, that he would always have someone to play baseball with, that he'd be there to teach him how to cast a fly rod. But there was little that she could say at all, little that he would understand.

A few days later, Hadley was making herself a cup of tea when she was surprised by the ring of the doorbell. She hadn't been expecting anyone, not even the parcel service. She was caught up on most of her design projects—a good thing since the creative juices hadn't at all been flowing lately. Through the kitchen window, she could see a splash of red signaling Aunt Margaret's sports car in the driveway. Today, she was almost grateful for one of her aunt's unannounced, spur-of-the-moment visits, rambling chatter notwithstanding. Feeling especially lonely, she had been craving the presence of another adult human being.

She put on a cheerful face and hurried to the front door.

The older woman, dressed in black Capri pants and a pale green silk shirt, greeted her with a hug.

"You're just in time for tea," Hadley said.

Aunt Margaret gave her a quick kiss on the cheek. She reached out to Nicky, but he ran behind the dining room table.

"What's up, Aunt Margaret?"

Having caught up with Nicky, she managed to leave a smudge of coral lipstick on his cheek. "I wanted to ask if you'd do some flyers for our hospital auxiliary bingo. Thelma Blassengame, who did them last year, moved to Florida. Her sister lives there, the one with six cats. Anyway, our publicity budget isn't very big, but we have some money to pay you."

"No need to pay me, Aunt Margaret. It's a good cause. All you have to pay for is the cost of printing the flyers."

The older woman gave her a perfumed hug. "That's sweet of you, dear. I'll get the information to you in a day or two."

"That will be fine."

"By the way, are you still in contact with Drake Matthieson?"

Hadley's heart skipped a beat. "No. Why?"

"Did you know he was engaged?"

Hadley's heart skidded to a stop and seemed to roll sideways off somewhere in her chest. "Where did you hear that?"

"My friend, Fred, who is the jeweler at Finklestein's—he's a very good dancer, by the way. You should see him do the mambo. Anyway, he said Drake came in this morning and looked over their complete selection of engagement rings."

Hadley's mouth went dry and her knees went wobbly. "I wasn't aware of that." She managed to keep her voice steady, but it still came out sounding like it belonged to someone she was overhearing in a different room.

"I never would have guessed," Aunt Margaret went on. "The chances of anybody getting him to the altar had to be about the same as a cow jumping over the moon. Maybe he's having a mid-life crisis. He's not all that far from forty, you know."

For a few seconds, Hadley couldn't say anything. "Please come in the kitchen." The invitation wasn't so much a show of hospitality as an overwhelming need to sit down.

The older woman took a seat by the window in the breakfast nook. Hadley put the kettle back on the stove and sat numbly across from her.

"Who do you suppose she is?" she asked.

Under the table, out of Aunt Margaret's view, Hadley clasped her hands in her lap to keep them steady. "I saw him at the carnival with a female firefighter. Her name was Melissa Giardelli."

"I don't believe I know her," she said, sounding mildly disappointed. She prided herself on knowing practically everyone.

Hadley got up and dropped a ball of Japanese green tea into a blue and white teapot and added the water from the kettle. She ended up spilling part of it. "Are you sure he's getting engaged? Maybe he was just doing some police work."

"Fred definitely got the idea it was personal."

Hadley felt a growing rawness in her throat. She'd been right. Kissing her had been merely recreational. It had meant nothing to him. No wonder it had been so easy for him to terminate their so-called friendship.

Struggling to look composed, she poured two cups of tea and

set them on the table, along with a small plate of cookies and a glass of milk for Nicky. She perched the boy up on a booster seat and sat next to him.

Aunt Margaret took a sip of tea. "You know, he has settled down quite a bit in the past few years. Past playboy reputation aside, Drake is a very good man. I'd trust him with my life's savings, modest though they be."

Hadley's teacup stopped before it reached her lips. "Just a few months ago, you were practically begging me to stay away from him. You said he was a hopeless Lothario."

"Well, I was wrong. Here he is, settling down. After the rough boyhood he had, marriage and family are probably what Drake needed all along."

"Dake," Nicky parroted. There were cookie crumbs on his cheek.

The lump in Hadley's throat swelled to the size of a baseball. It took a Herculean effort to keep her composure. Aunt Margaret looked at her watch. "Oh, dear, I have to meet Martha and Irene in twenty minutes. Publicity committee." She got up and gave Hadley a quick peck on the cheek. "Thanks for the tea and for doing the flyers. I'll be in touch. Call me if you need a baby-sitter."

"Thank you. I will."

Not trusting her ability to stifle her emotions much longer, she kept her seat instead of accompanying her aunt to the door. But the minute she heard the car door slam and the engine start, her eyes welled with tears.

She got up and went to the sink so Nicky wouldn't see. Outside the suddenness of it, Drake's engagement to Melissa made sense. Dedication to public service probably came first in both of their lives. They would understand each other perfectly.

She blotted her eyes with a dishtowel. There was nothing to

do but to keep on trying to get over him. So far, she hadn't made any progress at all.

After an all-but-sleepless night, Hadley awoke the next morning with pillow marks on her cheek, puffy eyes and a feeling of utter exhaustion.

She threw on her old denim overalls for some therapeutic Saturday-morning yard work and got breakfast. She'd been saving a frozen coffeecake for a special occasion. There didn't seem to be one anywhere on the horizon, and just for that reason, she got it out and popped it in the oven.

Then the phone rang. Expecting it to be Aunt Margaret, Hadley was surprised to hear what sounded like sobs on the other end of the line.

"Hadley, it's Lynn Murphy."

Hadley's stomach knotted. "Is there something wrong?"

"No, honey. I have the most wonderful news. Callie's coming home!"

For the first time in weeks, Hadley felt alive, as though her heart had stirred from a deep hibernation. "That's wonderful."

"I didn't tell you, but I had a journal I'd been keeping all these years. I poured my heart into it about my daughter. Well, I sent it to her, along with a letter. For weeks, I didn't hear anything. Then late last night, she called. I was so excited that I wanted to call you right away. But it was so late that I was afraid I'd wake you."

"I'm so happy for you, Lynn." Tears of a different kind formed in her eyes.

"She said that she now realizes that I really do love her. She said she didn't want to hurt me anymore, either."

Hadley wiped a tear from her cheek.

"She's coming next weekend," she gushed on. "She won't be here to stay, but at least I have my little girl back in my life. I'll never be able to repay you and the Lieutenant."

Hadley's stomach clutched at the reference to Drake.

"I've already been repaid. Give Callie my love."

Mrs. Murphy hung up amid a fresh wave of tears. Hadley's own joy was bittersweet because finding Callie was also a reminder of losing Drake.

Pulling herself together, she glanced into the living room where Nicky was watching cartoons. She took the coffeecake out of the oven and set the kitchen table for the two of them. But all the while, she thought of Mrs. Murphy and life's strange twists. Sorrow, in its slow and roundabout way, could turn to happiness.

After Quint, she couldn't imagine loving anyone again, but she had. And after Drake? It might be a long time in coming, but for every winter there was a spring. Only now, it seemed that it would never come.

Breakfast was ready. All she lacked was a toddler and the newspaper, which she'd forgotten to bring in from the porch. But when she opened the front door, her hand froze on the knob. Parked at the curb was a dark blue Jeep.

Her heart somersaulted. The newspaper lay untouched as she watched Drake emerge from the car. He started up the sidewalk toward her. "Good morning," he said, smiling crookedly. He was wearing a gray suit, a crisp white shirt and a teal green print tie. His hair was impeccably barbered; his shoes buffed to a glow.

"Drake, what are you doing here?"

At the sound of his name, Nicky came running from behind her onto the porch. Before Drake could get to the first step, Nicky tackled him around the knees.

"Hey, how's my buddy?" Drake asked.

Nicky craned his neck upward and grinned.

Hadley gently pulled Nicky back. "Drake, you shouldn't be

here. We agreed . . ." There was a catch in her throat. He looked so handsome. He had no right to do this to her.

"I just wanted to be sure you'd heard the good news about Callie."

For once, she wished he weren't so conscientious. "Yes, I just talked to her mother."

"Terrific, isn't it?"

"Yes." It hurt to even look at him, knowing that he belonged to someone else. She struggled to put on a brave show.

"Mrs. Murphy left a message for me at work. She also contacted the local police. They don't know much yet about Callie's story, but apparently various families took her in along the way. That's about all they could get out of Mrs. Murphy. She hadn't come back down to earth yet."

Hadley smiled at the thought of Mrs. Murphy suspended in the sky like some ethereal puppet. "Drake, you didn't need to go to all the trouble to come by."

"This wouldn't have happened without you," he said. "I wanted to see the smile it would bring to your face."

She felt an ache surrounding her heart. "Drake, please . . ."

"Hadley, I also came by because I want to talk."

"We've said everything. There's nothing else to say."

"Yes, there is. Could we go inside?"

Reluctantly, she led him into the kitchen where she pacified Nicky with a cup of juice.

"I know what you're going to say, Drake. I hope you and Melissa will be very happy."

A puzzled look came over his face. "Your good wishes are a bit premature. The date was a bust."

She stared at him, struggling to absorb what he'd said.

"The woman spent more time looking at herself in her compact than she did looking at me," he said. "What's more, she believes the pyramids were built by extraterrestrials and that the government is hiding the presence of aliens."

Hadley's mind slowly came out of its hard spin. "You're not engaged to her?"

A soft rumble of laughter came from his chest. "Where did you get that idea?"

"Aunt Margaret has a friend named Fred who works in a jewelry store."

He rolled his eyes. "I'll make a note to contact Fred the next time I need to send out an all-points bulletin."

"You weren't looking at diamonds?"

"Yes, but I'll explain in due time."

He took her wrists in his hands and her heart went wild.

"Don't feel bad about Melissa," she said. "Noland dusts off chairs before he sits in them. He also has a cucumber phobia."

Drake looked at her warily. "You didn't have a good time with him after all?"

She shook her head. "It wasn't going to work and we both knew it. It wasn't that he wasn't perfectly nice . . ."

He reached out and pulled her close. He touched his lips to her forehead, then the tip of her nose.

A lump rose to her throat. "Drake, I'm so afraid of you—afraid of us."

His gaze turned dusky. "Please don't be. I need you."

She looked at him, her heart on hold. Need wasn't the same as love.

"Something happened to me during that last raid. I'm certain that guy would have killed me if he'd gotten hold of my gun. He was so hyper that it took four of us to subdue him. During those moments I was struggling with him on the floor, all I could think about were you and Nicky and the possibility I'd never see you again."

She went weak. "You know that possibility will always exist. And I know it. I just don't know if I can deal with that again."

He took her firmly by the shoulders and held her at arm's length. "Hadley, this suit is my new uniform."

She blinked uncomprehendingly. "What do you mean?"

"I'm going into the detective division."

Hadley thought she was going to cry, but somehow managed to hold back her tears.

"The risk will be much lower, not that there won't be any. I could get a virtually risk-free desk job but that wouldn't guarantee the pipes overhead wouldn't break and wash me out the window. When it comes to life, there aren't any guarantees. Besides, I'm a cop, Hadley. And not being able to do what I love would be a form of death.

"I convinced myself that foregoing marriage and family was the noble thing to do considering the nature of my work. My job didn't scare me. But the thought of getting close to another human being did. So I became a master at keeping people— women in particular—at a safe distance. I was more afraid of commitment than anything I'd faced on the force. Even more, I was afraid of loving and then losing. There I'd be again, that thirteen-year-old boy alone in the world."

Hadley touched the sensuous curve of his bottom lip. "I don't want to lose anyone again, either. But I also know that I don't want to live without you."

He searched her face for a moment, his gaze like a caress. "I love you, Hadley. I want to spend the rest of my life with you. You and Nicky."

She burst into tears, this time tears of joy. "I want to spend my life with you. I love you, Drake. And Nicky loves you, too."

He kissed her with dizzying conviction, leaving her breathless.

His arms slid slowly from her shoulders and he picked up Nicky, who had begun pulling pots and pans out of the cabinet. Gradually, she began to come to her senses, realizing that nothing had been said about marriage.

With Nicky looking blissfully content in his arms, he strolled back toward her. Hadley knew that the picture of them together would remain forever in her mind.

"After what you've been through, I have no right to ask you this."

Her breath stalled in her chest as he took her hand and touched his lips to her fingers. He looked up, his gaze locking to hers.

"But will you marry me, Hadley?"

Her heart bounced as if it were on springs. "Yes."

With his free arm, he folded her and Nicky both into his embrace. "I took the biggest risk of my life coming here and putting my heart on the line. I had to do it, no matter what."

He kissed her lightly and then kissed Nicky. He shifted the boy to her arms.

"Stay where you are. I have something for you." He disappeared out the front door and came back, carrying three bouquets of long-stemmed red roses. He placed them in her arms and picked Nicky up again.

"Do you know why I got three dozen?"

She shook her head.

"To symbolize the three of us. And later, if you like, we can make it more."

"Yes," she said without a second of hesitation.

A look of total satisfaction crossed his face. "Let me put the best man down," he said, lowering Nicky to the floor. "I have something else."

Drake slipped a small black box from his inside pocket and handed it to her. "It's only a symbol of my intentions. Fred said you're free to exchange it for anything you like."

She opened the box and found a glistening solitaire mounted on a swirl of white gold. "It's perfect."

He slipped it on her finger and kissed her again, with a warmth and fervor that radiated all the way to her toes.

Nicky wandered back to the cabinets, noisily dragging out more pans. But no one noticed.

ABOUT THE AUTHOR

Bernadette Tabor Pruitt is a former newspaper reporter and college journalism instructor. She studied writing at the University of Oklahoma and is editor of and contributor to *The Salt of the Earth,* a series of profiles of Oklahomans who are among the last of their kind. Her interests include interior decorating, reading and traveling. She and her husband live in Wichita Falls, Texas, with a Shih Tzu named "Boo." *True Blue* is Bernadette's seventh romance novel.